# VOW to PROTECT

USA TODAY BESTSELLING AUTHOR
## J.L. BECK
NEW YORK TIMES BESTSELLING AUTHOR
## MONICA CORWIN

# 1

## VALENTINA

*I* know I should be more excited to attend my first party. Between dressing up and the fact that my fiancé, Sal, agreed to let my cousin and best friend, Rose, come along too, it's set to be a fantastic night. Rose isn't really interested in the party, but I fear leaving her alone in the house with my father or my fiancé, so I bring her as my plus-one.

They can be ruthless and sinister, plus I'm stronger than her. It's my duty to protect the only family I have left in this house.

I peer at my reflection in the mirror. The dress Rose chose for me hugs my curves, which only began filling out a few years ago. Not that there's much yet. I still feel like my small petite shape resembles an ironing board compared to Rose's curves and statuesque figure.

The champagne silk gown barely brushes the floor, Rose having hemmed it by hand all morning for me. It makes my pale skin shine in the mirror and sets off her own black cap sleeve number. We both look great, and I hug her to my side as she presses the last pin taming the unruly mass of brown known as my hair.

"Let's try to have some fun, okay?" I whisper.

She nods, meeting my eyes in the mirror. "Let's set a goal to make one sexy man trip over his feet tonight."

"Sal doesn't count." I snicker.

"Ugh, Sal isn't sexy. I know you're being conscripted to spend the rest of your life with him, but hopefully once you get married, he'll find a mistress to deal with his bullshit and leave you alone."

I snort. "A new goal then. Find a mistress for my future husband at this party. Someone we think he could go for after we get married."

It was a nice lie. But what are dreams? Nice lies to get you through the day, right?

We give each other one long conspiring look in the mirror and head downstairs for inspection by my father and Sal.

We descend to the foyer. Rose remains at my back, one step behind—not because she's inferior but because she's my support. My rock. The only thing keeping me from going apeshit most days.

My father steps out of his study, Sal follows, and they circle us like wolves. Once they finish scrutinizing us, my father sniffs, shakes his head, and points at the stairs. "Go back up to your room and change. You look like a cheap whore. I can see every inch of your body. You're supposed to be a respectful woman and set an example."

An example of what? What happens to women in this world when they can't stand on their own two feet? I know better than to question him, though I can't help but look down at the beautiful shimmering silk and frown at its loss. Instead of telling him off, I do the smart thing and say, "Yes, sir." Then I grab Rose's arm and haul her back up the stairs with me.

"Switch with your cousin," my father's hard voice calls after us. "At least she looks like a proper young lady."

I wince but continue walking, dragging Rose with me back to my bedroom.

"I hate those motherfuckers," she growls, throwing herself on the bed. I let out a half-hearted protest about her hair, but she turns her face to glare at me. "Do I look like I give a shit about my hair?"

I frown, looking down at the dress. "Let's just change, and then we can go. I'm sorry you worked so hard on my dress, and now I can't even wear it."

Rose sits up, twisting gracefully, and waves me away. "It doesn't matter. You're right. Let's change, and then we can get to drinking."

We swap dresses, and I have to help ease the zipper of mine up the side of her waist. It barely fits, and the length is a foot too short. I feel bad, but I'm not sure what else to do. I won't return to my father without this dress on. "Do you want to put on something else?"

She shakes her head. "We are already pushing it for time, and I'd expect if I went down in something else, then they'd order me right back up here out of spite. Or worse, make you go alone."

I hug her one more time and adjust her hair a little where a few stray pieces have fallen down her slim neck.

She meets my eyes, stilling my face in her hands. "If there is any way to get you out of this marriage, I'm going to find it. You deserve so much better than that asshole."

I nod, ducking my chin so she doesn't see the sheen of tears building in my eyes. "I know, but it's what Father wants, and you know I have to keep him happy."

"Not if we leave. How about at the party tonight, you and I just slip out the side door into the darkness? They'll never see us again. I have a little money saved, and you can sell some of your jewelry. We can get jobs and live a normal existence."

As wonderful as her dream sounds for us, I know it's useless to imagine. "You know if we did that, he would never stop looking for me. Both Sal and my father would hunt me down and drag me home. And then once they found me, they would kill me."

Rose sucks a ragged breath into her lungs and lifts my chin with her finger. "Don't say that."

"You don't think my father has been looking for a way to punish me all my life? Everything he does is to punish me for my mother's death. Everything. Sal is just another in a long list of things that suck about my life. I'm used to it by now." I pause, refusing to let myself get worked up over something that will never change. "We should go."

Rose looks like she wants to say more but doesn't. "I'll find a way, okay? Don't give up."

She wants to say more every time Sal says something hurtful or, worse, when he hits me to get his way. My father put my virginity up as a shield, but it doesn't protect me from Sal's fists.

I paste on the fake smile my father and Sal will expect to see me wearing and head toward the door. "Let's go before one of them comes up here after us."

Again, she trails me, and when we hit the foyer, it's only Sal in his tuxedo waiting for us. His black curls are slicked back, and he's altogether too oily and smooth. He always has been. I hated him the moment I laid eyes on him. He's a snake in the grass, waiting for the perfect opportunity to strike.

He holds out his elbow for me to take, and I wrap my arm around it. If I didn't, he'd drag me into him and make me pay for embarrassing him in front of Rose. It's a lesson I've learned many times from the palm of his hand.

The limo is waiting outside the house, and Sal opens the door for us. Rose climbs in first, and then he steps in front of me, slipping in so that he's stuck sitting between us. I wish I were the kind of person who had the balls to drag him out by his ear. Instead, all I manage is envisioning the squeak he'd make if I did it.

I buckle my seat belt, and the limo pulls away. Sal's cologne wafts off him in nauseating waves, but I don't dare roll down the window for air. He sees everything, and no matter what I do, it's all an insult to him. Every breath I take is an insult to him.

"I'm glad your father suggested you change. You look much more proper now. Although I do like the silk on you. Maybe you can put it back on for me later," he whispers.

I keep the disgust hidden from my tone. "If Father says it's alright."

I'm worthless in my father's mind, so he won't have me called a whore as well. In front of his friends, I'm the perfect doting daughter. There's no way for him to explain away rumors of my sleeping around to them, so he's forbidden Sal from touching me that way. I'll take it because the thought of him touching me intimately makes me want to scream.

He stiffens and leans away, taking the cloying scent with him. My father's one rule was no touching sexually before the wedding. And no matter how many times Sal has tried to coax me into breaking the edict, I don't. Not when it is the only life raft my father has ever provided.

Since I rebuffed him, Sal runs his hand up my thigh, squeezing so hard over the material I'll have a bruise. Unable to stop myself, I grab his hand and look him in the eyes. "He probably wouldn't like where that hand is either."

"Don't be such a little virgin," he hisses.

My virginity is the only thing keeping me safe from him, so I'll use it for a shield as long as I can. I know nothing about sex, and if the porn or the pictures Sal forces me to look at when my father is away are similar, I don't want anything to do with it. Even more so if he's with me.

Rose lets out a soft squeak across the car, and I glance over. Sal has his arm slung around her shoulders, and his lips are on her neck. Her eyes are blown wide and scared as she meets mine across the car. Despite her terror, though, her chin is tilted up, and she's trying to tell me she can take this. Take this for me. But God, I don't want her to, not when she shouldn't have to.

I grip his hand and return it to my upper thigh, drawing his attention back to me. When he turns to face me again, something tight breaks open in my chest, and I can breathe. "First, you don't want me, and now you think I'm ignoring you, Valentina. Make up your mind, babe."

I hate the way he says my name. The way he calls me babe as though it's affectionate. Every time I hear it, I want to throw up. But I can't, not with Rose in his clutches. "Sorry, we spent all this time getting ready. Don't you think I look nice?"

He lets his arm fall away from Rose and faces me fully. I almost sigh with relief. "You know you're beautiful. It's the only thing you've got going for you. That and your sweet honeypot I'm going to claim when we get married."

I barely stifle the gag which surges from my empty belly. Rose and I skipped dinner with my father and Sal, complaining we had too much to do to be ready for the party. Well, if I do vomit on him, then there won't be much of a mess.

"Thank you for the compliment," I manage after a moment. Thankfully, he doesn't notice my hesitation in answering.

"Our kids are going to be so hot," he says.

Another gag wells up inside me, and I have to turn my eyes away before he sees the disgust there. I know what kind of businesses he runs for his family. And the little side projects in human trafficking that keep him flush with cash.

Every Friday when my father goes to his meetings, Sal shows me videos. Clips of his men touchi—bile rises in my throat as I cut off the thought. I have to press the back of my hand to my mouth to ensure nothing comes up. It was bad enough when I thought he only dealt in grown women.

My hands are shaking, and I wrap them around my waist. His eyes narrow, but as he opens his mouth, the car jerks to a halt outside a high-rise building.

For a second, he stares out the window and then nods. "We're here. Get the fuck out so we can make our entrance together."

Gladly. I shove the door open and take a deep breath of the clean night air. Until he curls a proprietary arm around my waist and leads me toward the building. Rose trails us. We lock eyes for a second, her asking if I'm okay while I do the same with her. We both nod and focus on the mission: have a tiny bit of fun without riling Sal too much.

The foyer of the building is lovely. Decorated in creams and maroon with a sparkling crystal chandelier hanging in front of a bank of elevators.

Inside the elevator, a man in a uniform nods and presses the button I assume is for the party. Sal's arm locks around me tighter the higher we climb.

"Don't embarrass me tonight," he says, his eyes on the number panel as we ascend. "Either of you. Or I'll make you regret it."

Rose and I once again lock eyes behind his back in a moment of solidarity. We can do this.

The elevator opens to a beautiful glittering crowd milling about a grand foyer. The white marble floor has matching marble columns that line the edge of the circular space. We squeeze past couples until we spot the open doorway to a large ballroom. Inside, tables skirt a small dance floor as servers carrying tinkling trays of champagne flutes weave through the throng.

Sal releases me and smooths his hair back. "Find a table and wait for me. If I see you talking to another man, I'll kill him."

## 2

## ADRIAN

The only thing I hate more than parties are parties where everyone is considering the best way to kill me.

I can almost see the yearn to maim and dismember in their eyes as they pass me with little dips of their chin. Every single one of us is a liar. And the party to open the season makes us all a hundred times worse.

This year, it's my turn to host the opening gala. As if sparkle and glam could negate the blood that would hit the streets in short order. Likely before the first guests leave for the evening.

The heavy weight of a palm clamping my shoulder makes me tense up until Kai, my second, comes around into my field of vision. "Ready for this, old man?"

I wince. "Cut out the old man shit. I'm only a few years older than you."

He grins, all gleaming white teeth. "But about ten years older than all the little girls these mommies and daddies are throwing at you. I hear whispers they want to find you a queen."

And not a single one of them will know I'm looking for one myself. Otherwise, I'm vulnerable to both preying mothers and scheming fathers on all sides. Until I secure a bride, my father's empire won't officially be mine in the eyes of these people.

"Keep your eyes and ears open, Kai. I have a bad feeling about tonight."

His hand tightens on my shoulder. "You have a bad feeling about every party we go to, boss."

He isn't wrong.

A pretty little blonde makes eyes at Kai from across the room. Then when her gaze slides to mine, she loses her nerve. "Someone wants you," I point out to him.

"Who doesn't?" he parries.

I shrug him off my shoulder. "Don't get distracted. You and the men need to stay alert."

He gives me a wink and saunters toward the blonde. Despite his nonchalance, I know he won't let his guard down. His ease has always been an act he uses to play a role, so they don't realize what he really is until it's too late.

My other five closest soldiers, six counting Kai, have spread out throughout the room to listen, watch, and guard my back. But it will take a lot more than their presence to put me at ease here. At least this year, I decided to host it on neutral ground. The Holland Hotel, owned and operated by an anonymous, unaligned individual, is the site for all inter-territory meetings. So it makes sense they would host the gala too. And this year, I won't find someone trying to sneak their way past security or hack my computer networks.

As I watch each person walk past me, I can't help but see the lies spewing from their mouths. Each syllable spoken in sweet smiles, all greasy with every untruth, turns my stomach. If I'm going to kill someone, I have the decency to at least tell them outright.

The neck of my perfectly tailored tux feels too tight, like a noose around my neck.

"Scowl any harder, and people will start running for their weapons," a sweet voice says as she approaches. My fifth wears red satin tonight, cut so low that I would be about to see her belly button with another inch. Another weapon my soldiers employ effortlessly: their beauty.

"Andrea." I scan the crowd. "Where's your twin?"

She rolls her neck, her black hair sliding over the bare curve of her shoulder. "Oh, he's around here somewhere. Probably getting himself into trouble."

"Shouldn't you be joining him?" I say, keeping my gaze on the slow amble of the people around me. I half wish someone would start something so I could get the hell out of here.

"I will soon enough. See anyone I should keep my eye on?" Her focus returns to the crowd as well now.

I shake my head. "Not yet. I'll let you know if I see something. Go play and be nice."

She saunters back into the fray, and I snag a passing glass of champagne. I don't usually drink because I feel out of control when I have too much. And no one can see me like that. But Andrea is right. If I continue scowling from the fringes of the ballroom, it won't help me find the woman I need to turn into my wife.

But I'm not the only one who's counting the seconds until it's socially acceptable to leave. A young woman in black with a mass of barely restrained curls stands near a table with someone else I don't recognize. Which is impossible since I know every member of our little twisted society.

Then I catch sight of Sal squeezing through the crowd, not even bothering to be sly at the way he ogles the women he passes.

When he reaches the table, the girl in black stiffens and shifts away from him but then allows the fucking dickhole to drag her by the arm to his side again. And he isn't gentle about it either. I'm three seconds from grabbing his threadbare tux and allowing Andrea to escort him out. She loves nothing more than showing a man like him what she thinks of his kind.

So he succeeded in buying himself a family name. And by the size of the rock on Rachel—Royal—no, I can't remember her name, her daddy had to buy it for her fiancé to propose. Sal and her father, Victor, have been in business together a long time. When word started to spread about his engagement to Novak's daughter, I thought they were sampling their own product. Now, seeing the way he handles her as though he owns her, I believe it.

And I want to fucking kill him for the way he's touching her.

For the sadness I see that isn't quite masked by her bright smile.

My stomach roils, and I shift my focus away before I do something stupid. She isn't mine, and interfering will only cause trouble. Seeing that look in her eyes—the same look my mother used to wear—unnerves me in a way I haven't been in a long time.

My mother was the only truly good female I've ever known. Even Andrea, one of my closest friends, is a bitch on a good day.

I realize I'm staring at her again. The black dress looks a little loose on her petite frame, and she's young. She's so fucking young someone probably should have carded her at the door. Too young to have the weight of the world written in her gaze.

The urge to find out what color her eyes are overtakes me, and I slowly shift around the ballroom, smoothly avoiding people trying to capture my attention. When I finally make it to the right angle, the lighting is too dark for me to tell, but staring at her straight on, with Sal's hand inching toward her ass, I can clearly see how much she hates him.

A puzzle then. Why would one of the society's pampered princesses marry her daddy's business partner if she didn't like him? She, like me, should have her choice of suitors. Her hair is a thing of beauty, piled up on her head in a mass of natural curls. A flash of what all that black silk would look like spread over my white sheets starts a craving I won't be able to quench.

No. She doesn't belong to me. I try to shake off the longing, the stark desire that shoves its way between my ribs and nestles in deep. It doesn't budge, especially when she delicately lifts her champagne glass, and I watch her pretty pink lips cup the rim.

Instantly, I see her on her knees, that dress pooled around her slim waist, her curls tangled between my fingers as she takes my dick down her throat. It's an obscene fantasy. Especially because she looks like she's never even been kissed properly. A likely scenario given her fiancé.

Fuck. I can't stay here staring at her all night. Someone is bound to notice, and it will paint a target on her back.

I tear my eyes away and duck through the crowd, intent on putting some distance between us. If she came closer to me and I caught her delicate scent, I'd lose my fucking mind and start a war I'm not prepared to win yet. Because when I go into battle, nothing will be left standing but me and my five. She'd be collateral damage. Damage her father likely would consider insignificant if he cares so little of her to give her away to that asshole.

The balcony calls my name. It's empty, and I spot Ivan, my second lieutenant, taking up position on the other side of the doors. The privacy after being stuck in a crowded ballroom for an hour is a welcome relief. The traffic sounds from below barely reach this high, so it's nothing but the cold cut of the wind, which I appreciate after the stifling heat inside.

I allow myself a moment to wonder who might have followed me out here and attempted to toss me over the edge if Ivan hadn't been tailing me. My father had many enemies, and now, I seem to have inherited them. People I barely know hate me for my father's actions. If they only knew what having me for a real enemy would be like.

But this party opens the season, and for the next three months, every single person here must watch their back. The season-opening signals movement in society. Movement bought with blood, criminal activity, and good old-fashioned murder. Then anything goes until the final party of the season. Afterward, a mandatory nine months of peace allows the new fault lines to be drawn. Anyone who violates it meets justice at the hand of every ruling family. No one has ever survived the gauntlet.

My own father certainly didn't. Thankfully, once they took his life, his sins washed down the drain with his blood. It didn't matter that he'd become too old to even understand his actions in the end—they showed him no mercy. And soon, they will learn what my mercy looks like.

Almost involuntarily, I turn back to the doors and peer around Ivan's shoulder through the glass. She's still standing beside Sal, who is getting drunker by the minute. The other girl with her has the hard cut of fear in her eyes as she watches Sal and his fiancée. I don't know why that fear eats at something inside me, but it blooms my own batch of fear for the innocent on Sal's arm.

I open the doors and step back in, letting the last of the night air cool my back before closing the door again.

Ivan melts back into the crowd, and I watch her. I want to know what her voice sounds like. What color her eyes are. I want to know what kind of words she uses when she begs.

Most of all, I want Sal's blood pooling across the concrete so he won't ever touch her again.

I shove past a few society members, intent on reaching their table to introduce myself, but someone catches my arm. I spin with a curse and glare down into the eyes of Madeline Cerny, heiress to the biggest blow empire in the country. And by the way she wobbles in her two-thousand-dollar shoes, she's been sampling her product.

I try to keep my tone even as I address her. "Can I help you, Maddie?"

She bats her eyelashes, or I think she does. It's more like a wink gone wrong, but I remain the gentleman.

She, however, has lost her damn mind. I realize this when she reaches out and grabs my cock as if she has permission to touch me. As if she even has permission to speak to me.

I don't get the pleasure of ripping her claw-tipped fingers off before Alexei, Andrea's twin, is there, leading her away.

With disgust, I stare after them. Then I remember my mission before she mauled me. I spin to find the flower amongst the weeds. But she's disappeared.

# 3

## VALENTINA

*I*f this is what the rest of my life looks like, I don't want it. Every person at this party is either drunk, high, or both. And not in the glamorous, I'm rich so I can do anything I want sort of way. They are all sloppy and mean, and I'm about to lose my shit if Sal touches me one more time.

Rose meets my eyes for a moment, conveying her own distress that Sal has barely left us alone for a second. We'd hope to be drinking and watching the people we've never gotten to meet. But we can barely even speak with Sal breathing down the neckline of my dress as if he'd dropped his keys in there.

A part of me wishes my father had come tonight. He gave his excuses, saying Sal was within his rights to come in his stead since he would soon be his son-in-law. If he were here, he would witness Sal's clear disregard for the sexual contact rule and maybe, for once, do something to help me. Maybe he'd pretend I'm his daughter and not his burden.

Since Rose is only related by marriage, he does consider her a burden. Her mother, my mother's sister, died along with my mom, and we've been inseparable ever since. I suspect my father knows that if he throws Rose out, there is nowhere in the world I won't go to find her. To protect her. She may be my cousin by blood, but she's my sister in every way that matters.

The thoughts of my father showing any kind of support for me are nothing more than a silly fantasy I nurtured as a child. My mother died before I reached the tween years, and after that, well, the darkness that clung to my father before became all-consuming. My mother's light tempered him. Without her, he has no conscience. No soul. And since it's my fault my mother is gone, I have to try to be that for him. Even when it earns me bruises more often than patience.

Sal laughs at something one of his greasy friends says. The same friend who latched on to Rose the second he joined our table. I need to find a way to rescue us both. Get us home before Sal gets too drunk to remember he cedes to my father until we marry.

I gently peel Sal's hand from my waist and give him a smile. "I'll be right back. Just going to powder my nose."

Rose takes the hint and squeezes away from the handsy guy whose name I don't bother to remember.

We link our arms and press into the crowd before Sal can think to call us back. The bathroom is likely the only safe place for us right now. We make a beeline across the marble foyer and past the elevators to the little alcove that indicates the restrooms. The facilities are just as lovely as the ballroom. I'm impressed by the velvet sitting room and the crystal chandeliers in front of each solid wood door leading to the toilets.

I don't actually need to go, but Rose does and rushes into one of the little rooms while I take a seat on a dove gray settee. My feet are already aching from these shoes, and I feel like Sal's hand has made a permanent mark on the curve of my waist. Like the ghost of a pool's water after a long day of swimming.

I wait for Rose but catch the sound of raised voices outside the door to the ladies' room. Worrying it's Sal about to embarrass me, I rush out of the room to intercept him before he can storm in to find me.

But it's not Sal standing in the foyer. It's an impossibly tall man in a very expensive black-on-black tuxedo, and he looks pissed. He's watching a man and a woman in red lead another woman to a stairwell, but it appears the other woman doesn't want to go. I'm about to say something, but when I focus on the other man again, he's moved several feet closer to me—like only a few inches separate us. I catch the notes of his cologne, something smoky maybe with a hint of ginger.

He smells good. Like really good. I swallow and duck my chin, about to try to make a graceful exit, but he gently lifts my gaze to his with his index finger under my chin.

"What's your name?"

I swallow so I don't squeak when I answer him. With his eyes locked on mine, I can't even think straight. He towers over me, taking up the space both around him and around me, but unlike Sal, it feels like he owns that space, and I'm the interloper.

"Valentina Novak," I offer.

He doesn't say his name, only studies my face, his finger our only point of contact. I want to tuck my cheek so I can press my nose to his pulse point and get a good whiff of him.

Like a damn serial killer.

"What is this look on your face for, Val?"

Val. I blink. No one has ever called me anything other than Valentina or Miss Novak. Well, except Sal, but his names are curses and don't count.

"You smell good."

His forehead bunches up as he watches me. His dark hair is styled with a soft wave; it even looks like it would be soft to run my fingers through. Sal favors gel that turns his hair into a helmet. Not that I would want to touch it.

This man, though, there are a lot of things I want to do. And I don't understand why. We don't know each other. And while he is very beautiful, he must be fifteen years older than me. Apparently, I have a thing for older men now.

He's still silent, and I let him hold my chin even though it's a dangerous game with Sal likely about to discover us at any moment.

"Did you just say I smell good?" he asked. His deep and smoky voice has a hint of incredulity that is sweet, exactly like his scent.

"What did you want me to do? Lie?"

"Most would. Many here would make something up or deliver a stinging remark meant to gain the upper hand."

I shake my head, and it dislodges my chin from his grasp. He drops his arm slowly as if he's reluctant to stop touching me.

"No. I've had enough malice in my life. I refuse to give it back to others. Are you alright? I saw those people dragging someone away. Did she try to hurt you?"

His frown deepens, and he gently shakes his head. "Not hurt me, no. She only succeeded in embarrassing herself in front of a room full of people. However, I can't let the insult pass. She was removed, and that will be enough unless she tries again."

I shrug and smile. "Seems fair. I'd want to throw a woman out if she grabbed my genitals too."

A short laugh bursts out of him, and his smile...good lord...that smile is like staring directly into the sun. There are dimples, his five o'clock shadow, the straight white edge of his teeth, and those full lips, can't forget those.

"You saw that, did you?"

I give him a smile back, a real one that I could feel on my forehead. "Of course, I just didn't realize who she was until I thought about it some more."

The click of heels from the bathroom brought Rose in line with my back. I glance at her over my shoulder, but her face has taken on a pallor I only see when Sal is drunk and forward with her.

"Valentina," Rose whispers. "We should get back."

Her eyes are locked on the man, who is significantly more rigid and forbidding now that someone else is with us.

Dipping down, he captures my hand, brushes his soft lips over my knuckles, and releases me. It takes less than a second, yet I'll be replaying it in my mind for the next year.

"It was a pleasure to meet you, Val. I hope to see you again soon." He tugs a black card from his pocket and presses it into my hand. The only thing on it is a phone number embossed in gold. "If you need anything, call this number and ask for Adrian."

"Adrian," I intone, still memorizing his features.

Rose pulls me away, and I let her, stumbling slightly as I shove the card into my clutch. We skirt the edge of the crowd until we reach an alcove, then Rose spins me to face her and clasps my face between her hands. "Are you okay?" Her voice is frantic, panicky, and thick.

I bat her fingers from my face. "No, what? No. Why are you freaking out right now? Adrian was very nice to me."

Her eyes are huge, and she still hasn't regained her color. "That man is a monster. The monster. The head of the Doubeck family. If you think marrying Sal is bad...that man will chew Sal up and eat him for breakfast. He's not someone you fucking make friends with, Valentina."

I shake off her hands and take a deep breath. Every second he and I spent talking about nothing felt meaningful. Thick with tension and possibility. A low ache has taken root in my belly and springs to life when I think about him.

"You're overreacting. He was nice to me. And he didn't hurt the woman who basically molested him in front of the entire party." And we both know I don't use that word lightly, considering some of the things Sal has forced us to bear witness to.

She shakes her head. "I don't know what happened between you but don't think about him again. He will get you killed, tortured, and tossed out like trash. Just be careful. If he tries to talk to you again, be nice, but get away as fast as you can."

"That is ridiculous. He's not some monster lying in wait to chew me up."

She shakes her head, something else in her eyes now, and she spins me to face the crowd. Across the room, Sal is leaning against a column, and his eyes are locked on us. There's nothing kind there, nothing curious or open. The only thing I see in Sal's eyes when I look at him is death. "Him, on the other hand?" I say, tugging her along with me as I head toward him. "I wouldn't be surprised if he tried to murder me the second after I say 'I do.'"

When I reach him, he grips my arm hard and sets a punishing pace to the elevators. I guess the party is over. I try to look around, hoping I'll see Adrian one more time before we leave. No doubt this will be our last party if Sal saw us talking. And the hatred on his face tells me he did. He can't kill Adrian, but he can certainly hurt me enough that I won't try to talk to anyone else ever again.

No sooner than the elevator doors close around us does the back of his hand hit my cheek. And the blow is hard. I can feel the indent of his knuckles where they made contact with my cheekbone. I do nothing more than cup the stinging spot and stare straight ahead. Breathe and don't enrage him further. Those are the words I live by, and the words that have saved my life more times than I can count. And as long as his attention is locked on me, he will leave Rose alone. She's the only reason I've stayed in that house. I can pretend it's for my father's sake all I want, but I do it for her. My best friend. My only family.

We reach the foyer, and I drop my hand to quickly pull some curls to cover the red welt I spot in the shiny elevator doors. He drags me through the people and furniture outside. Once the driver opens the limo door, he shoves me in. Rose goes around to the other door.

When the car pulls away, I brace for the next strike, and like always, he delivers. Except I expect another slap. I don't expect the punch that hits solidly on my orbital bone. Blackness overtakes me before I even feel the pain.

# 4

# ADRIAN

From the moment I climb out of bed to the moment I'm standing in the shower with the hot water beating down my back, I'm thinking about my little Val.

My little Val. I don't know how I'll accomplish it yet, but I always get my way in the end. And if killing her bastard of a fiancé and coward of a father is what it will take to make it happen, then...it'll be fucking Christmas.

The crystal clear gray of her eyes comes back to me. There was no guile in them when she talked to me. Hell, I didn't even think she knew who I was when I told her my name. It had been a very long time since I met a woman who awakens me the way she does.

I hang my head and stare down at the hot marble under my feet. My cock has been aching since I got out of bed, and I suspect if I don't do anything about it now, it will continue to rise every time Val's pretty eyes or sexy mouth spring to my mind.

I grip my dick roughly and give the head a squeeze. No, she wouldn't touch me like this.

She'd have to use both her delicate hands to work me. But she wouldn't touch me to hurt me. The innocence written in every line of her body told me she'd touch me to explore, to witness, and watch how to make me come apart for her. That's the kind of power the innocent crave. Not pain and torture, but pleasure and peace. It's the peace men like me grow addicted to. It's the peace I see in her face when I look at her. It's the peace making me fuck my hand in my own goddamn shower right now.

I continue pumping my fist up and down my length while I tease my senses with the little hints of Val she gave me last night. The soft soap scent wafting from her skin. No perfume, barely any makeup, and that fucking hair.

I groan, pumping faster now as I imagine my fingers twisting in the strands, brushing it from her face while I fuck her tight hot body. Again, I picture her unbound length spread across my white sheets and waking up with it draped across my chest and her thighs between mine. How she'll look at me in wonder while I lick her cunt for the very first time. Because I know fucking Sal hasn't been doing a damn thing to pleasure her during their engagement. In fact, I doubt she's ever had a man between her thighs.

A fucking virgin. The thought makes me shoot my load on the marble, and I spend longer than usual pumping myself as I come down from the fantasy. When I release myself, I'm thinking about the innocent smile she gave me and realize I'm back to fucking peace.

She will belong to me one day, but I'll never be able to have peace. Not while my mother's killer is still alive. And not while I have an entire society to bring to heel under my control. My father managed it effortlessly until his age got the better of him, but I'm not quite ready to earn my crown in a river of blood. Maybe after I claim Val and Christmas comes early.

The thought of her fiancé's blood spilling across black concrete chases away the sour mood I felt building. I usually didn't take joy in killing. If

I had to do it, I had to do it, but him...no, I'd be more than fucking happy to insert a bullet into his pervert of a brain and then watch him shit himself as he dies.

I grab the towel off the rack, then quickly dry off and dress before stepping out of my suite in the hall. The maids have already been through, but I hear the murmur of someone toward the dining room of my penthouse condo.

Breakfast should have been finished hours ago. When I enter the room, I find Kai, my best friend and the leader of my unruly band of enforcers, talking on the phone. He's speaking Portuguese too fast for me to keep up.

When I step into the room, he quickly ends his call and shifts to face me. "Did you talk to Novak's daughter last night?"

I take the seat beside him at the round glass table and survey the black suit he's wearing today. "Ermenegildo, is it? Do I pay you enough to afford a thirty-thousand-dollar piece of fabric?"

"Ari," he says, his tone edged with reproach. He's the only one who can call me by the name I used as a child—the name she called me. And he's the only fucking one who can use that tone of voice when he says it.

"It wasn't as if I planned to speak to her. She stepped out of the restroom when the twins were escorting someone out of the stairwell. Would you prefer I ignore her and make a scene?"

His eyes narrow. "The way I hear it, you did make a scene when you kissed her knuckles in front of her fiancé."

Back to fucking Sal, and my good mood evaporates into nothing. "Oh, did the big bad child trafficker call to tattle on me?"

Kai sits back, his dark skin catching the light from the window on the far side of the room. "We can't move on Novak yet. If you rile Viktor and his partners, it might change something that we won't be able to account for in enough time to adjust the plans." Now he's calm, using a tiger tamer voice as if it will keep me from marching out the door and dumping Sal into oncoming traffic.

A maid comes into the room carrying a tray of coffee, and I snag a mug as she sets it between us. When she leaves again, I meet Kai's eyes. "I told you it meant nothing. Now drop it. If Sal is upset, well, he should know better than to make a fuss. The fact that he doesn't know better worries me more than anything. Usually weasels like him have a strong sense of self-preservation. If he feels confident, then there has to be a reason he feels that way."

Kai takes a sip of his own coffee. "He is about to marry Novak's daughter. Maybe he thinks Novak's position in the society will shield him?"

I shrug and slick back the wet curls from my face. Eventually, it will dry that way and stay in place, but for now, it pisses me off. But not enough to take ridicule from one of my five for asking them to buy me a blow dryer. Maybe I'll shave it off and be done with it.

I wonder if Val would like my head shaved. She seemed interested in my hair as she scanned my features last night. No. I force my focus back to Kai.

"He thinks he's safe for now. And maybe he is. We can't move, and I doubt many are strong enough to take on Novak's operations. For this season, at least, he might be safe," I say. But the words taste disgusting in my mouth. I hope that dickhole never feels a day of safety again. If only for the sadness I spotted in Valentina's eyes last night.

"What else do you have?" I prompt, then take another sip of my coffee. "Any fallout from the party last night? Any new battle lines drawn in blood this morning?"

He shakes his head. "It's been a relatively quiet morning. I sent the five out to do a little digging in all the territories. See if they can pick up anything we might want to know about. I sent the twins to Novak's territory since Alexei is the most levelheaded of that lot, and Andrea will never risk his safety."

"Tell them to come and talk to me when they return. I want a personal report."

He nods and then sits and watches me, saying nothing.

"What, Kai? If you are going to bring up Sal again, I'm going to punch you in the dick hard enough you won't be any use flirting at the casinos tonight."

"It's not about him. No, I'm just worried about you."

My heart rolls over in my chest, but it doesn't show on my face. He knows I've been hunting for a wife, and the woman who stands by my side, who becomes my queen, has big shoes to fill. My mother is the only woman I've ever loved, and the only woman I've ever cared about losing.

"Why? I'm confident I'll make an alliance this season or next, and then we won't have to worry anymore."

"You might be confident, but I'm not. Hell, you scare most women away with just a glance. Last night, people were walking to the other end of the room so they didn't have to cross your path to get to the bar."

I shrug. "When have I ever been the sort of man who puts people at ease, tell me that? How is it news to any of you that finding someone I can trust who puts up with my very special level of insanity is going to be a difficult task?"

My mother's death had broken something inside me. Inside my father too, not that he ever showed that pain to me. Now, I live to take his place and do it better, build things stronger, strong enough that when I'm old and gray, no one will dare put a knife in my back.

"Maybe you need to get laid. You want me to call that girl from the casino you like?"

"No. I don't want you to find someone to get my dick wet. I want you to do your fucking job and give me a way to bring down Novak, and soon."

For a second, I entertain the idea of going to the casino, hunting down a girl with wild curls and a petite frame to slack this knife in my gut. But even the thought of it feels like a betrayal to her. A betrayal. To a fucking woman I have no claim over. At least not yet.

No. I won't do that. Because when I look her in the eye and tell her she belongs to me, I want to believe it, and I want her to know it as fact.

Kai shoves out of the chair and buttons his jacket. "For the record, since you asked, I won this suit off one of the Italians in a card game a month ago. He stripped it off right there at the table."

I couldn't help but smile at that. "Were you playing strip poker with one of the Italian boys, Kai? What would your mother think?"

His turn to smile now. "She'd think I was crazy for walking away from his lambo in favor of a few yards of fabric."

I study him from the tip of his polished shoes to his short immaculate haircut. "She wouldn't be wrong, but you do look good, man. If you head to the casino, make sure everything is ready for the fight next week. I don't want any issues, and I don't want anyone thinking they can rig our system."

With a nod, he takes his coffee, his phone, and his iPad with him as he walks out. A few minutes later, the front door slams, and the alarm activates behind him with a sharp chime.

Immediately, my thoughts zero back on Val. I wish I'd been able to talk to her longer last night. Spend a few minutes more listening to her talk and studying her.

Fuck.

I shove back the chair and stalk out of the room toward my office. For now, I need to put her out of my mind. The upcoming fight I'm hosting at my casino is an inter-society event, which is always fraught with danger during the season. I have shit to do, and it doesn't involve mooning over some girl who will be mine soon enough.

No matter how fucking beautiful she is.

## 5

## VALENTINA

*A* week after the party, the bruise on my face has finally shifted to a nasty yellow shade. The yellow shade is easier to cover with concealer, so I can finally stop hiding in my room. The last time I showed my father the bruises Sal left on me, he called me disgusting and told me I probably deserved it. I don't want to encourage Sal further with my father's approval.

I haven't been able to stop thinking about Adrian and what Rose called him. *A monster.* And I spent a lot of my time lying in bed over the past few days, wondering if he's the kind of monster other monsters fear.

A plan forms in my mind, but it's half-baked at best. I want to talk to Rose about it, but she's been avoiding me since the party, and since I haven't been able to leave my room much, I haven't figured out why.

I finish dressing in comfortable jeans and a T-shirt. My father is out of town for the next week, so at the very least, the reprieve will mean I get to talk to Rose, and we won't have to see Sal very much.

When I enter the small dining room for breakfast, it's empty. There is food on the table, though, so I help myself to bacon and toast, then grab the newspaper someone left there earlier.

By the grease stains on the edge of it, and the fact that only a few pieces of bacon are left, I can tell my luck has turned, and Sal is in the house somewhere. If I sneak back to my room after I eat, maybe I won't have to see his greasy face.

Instead of lingering, I take the paper and my plate up to my room and lock the door. So far, it's kept him out of my space, that and the hefty fear of my father's reaction if he discovered him inside. It seems he's fine with Sal's bruises but draws the line at premarital sex—thank freaking goodness.

I settle in a chair by my favorite bookcase and balance the plate on my knee while I scan the newspaper. The name of a new casino pops out at me, and I read the article. It's a puff piece about the restaurants and the great bar service, but I thought I remembered my father talking about an underground society fight being held there soon. Tonight maybe?

I stare at the door and wonder if I can sneak into my father's office without Sal seeing me. He'd have written something down about it if he planned to attend. And a place like that seems exactly where a girl might find herself a monster-eating monster.

I finish up my toast and re-read the article for any information that might help me. It doesn't give me anything useful, but it does give me a few minutes to bolster myself into going back downstairs to rummage through my father's office.

Rose usually helps me do these things. She runs interference with the house staff or plays lookout when necessary. Not that I steal into his office often for information. Well, not recently when I might encounter my fiancé.

Mentally, I should prepare myself for it to actually happen. It would be the easiest thing, the most acquiescing all around. Yet every time I have to consider Sal as my fiancé, I want to puke. I also have very little doubt that once my usefulness to him wears off, he'll kill me with his own two hands.

Even then, I'm sure my father will find a way to blame me for it.

I fold the newspaper and sit my plate on top of it. Then head back down the stairs. A quick glance along the hallway reveals it's empty, and I sigh heavily, my shoulders falling away from my ears.

I cross the hardwood floor to the double doors of my father's office and slip inside. Usually, when he's not in residence, he keeps them locked, but if he has to go out of town for longer than a day, he won't just in case one of his associates needs to get inside for something.

As always, the place is immaculate. The staff are ordered to dust daily, and if even one tiny thing is out of place, my father freaks out. I've been on the receiving end of one of those hissy fits many times. The cook calls him particular, but that's because she gets paid double what she would make anywhere else to deal with his crap. I can't complain either because she is good at her job.

I rummage through the drawer he usually keeps a spare calendar in, but it's not there. He must have taken both his usual calendar and the spare on his trip. Which means something is going on I probably don't want to know about.

Feeling a little down about not finding my prize, I glance around the room and give it one more half-hearted search for anything that might give me a clue about the casino or the fight.

I knew I had a direct line to Adrian himself. But Rose insisted he was dangerous, and I don't want to disregard her opinion. If I attend the fight, I can see what kind of man he is and then retreat or approach with more information.

With nowhere left to look, I sit in one of the leather club chairs across from my father's desk to think. So what if Adrian is more dangerous than I imagined when we first met? Isn't he the kind of man who might be able to do some damage to a guy like Sal? The only thing I couldn't abide was roping Adrian in to help me and then getting him hurt or worse. Thanks to my father, Sal is making powerful friends in the society. The thought of never seeing Adrian again because of Sal shoots a burn through my chest I don't understand.

It's also not something I can entertain. Not when I'm about to be married off to a psychopath.

The police are always another option. But after the one time my father brought the police chief to dinner, and they spent hours talking, I crossed that exit strategy off my list of options.

Rose suggested more than once I do it myself. My father wouldn't allow me to go to prison since it would sully his name and bring him under scrutiny from many sides. I just don't have the heart to tell her I'm not strong enough. Not my best friend who endures so much by staying here with me when all she wants to do is run.

I know she stays because she loves me. And I stay because I haven't quite given up hope that my father will return to the loving, doting man he was before we lost my mother.

Everything changed after her death—everything—and now I lay awake at night seeing the dead eyes of the woman he shot in the street a few weeks after it happened. I watched my mother die, and then I watched this woman, who didn't look much older than my own mother, die as well. Her blood ran into the sewer drain, and I watched it mix with the rain until my father pulled me away.

Ever since then, I've been afraid to look at a gun, or a knife, or anything that wanders into these walls strapped to my father's associates. Once Sal realized my fear of guns, he likes to press them to my face to get my attention. And worse, to Rose's.

I'm about to leave my father's office and hide out in my room with my demons when I hear a muffled groan from the door adjacent to my father's office. I wait, frozen, and listen for a few more seconds until it happens again. Definitely a masculine groan. Am I about to walk in on a couple of staff members sleeping together?

Well, better me than the cook, or they will both be fired. I bolster myself to break things up so they can get back to work and don't get into trouble. Then I shove the door open and blink to try to understand what I'm seeing.

It's not servants.

It's Sal.

And Rose.

She's pressed over the edge of the desk Sal uses when he works with my father. Her skirt is bunched around her hips, and Sal is pumping into her from behind.

I'm not jealous. Please, who the hell would be jealous of someone taking him away from me. But it's not him I'm watching. It's her. And the dead-eyed look she's wearing like the woman in the alley. Like my mother. Except she's breathing, moving even. Struggling. She's struggling.

Everything snaps into focus as clear as day, and I start moving before I can think. My fist connects solidly with Sal's cheek, and he rears back as pain surges up my arm. But it throws him off enough that he releases Rose, and she can maneuver around the desk to stand behind me. She's a foot taller, but I don't care. Right now, I'd rip him apart with my teeth if I have to in order to protect her.

"What the hell do you think you're doing?" I demand. "You can't fuck me, so you rape my cousin?"

He glares tucking himself back into his pants before taking a menacing step forward. "She wanted it. And your father gave us permission, so go ahead and tell him you caught us together. He won't give a shit."

He tests the skin on his cheek and takes another step toward me. I hold my ground and spread my arms to block his view of Rose. "You touch her again, and I'll kill you."

This time, he laughs at me. A loud sniffling guffaw and then he spins around the room like it's all a joke. "You, tiny little Valentine, think you can kill me?"

His face becomes serious, and he pulls a black handgun from a holster under his arm. "How are you going to do that when you can't even look at a gun?"

He's right. Even now, I can't stand the sight of it. I almost throw up my toast when he pushes the barrel against my lips and forces it against my teeth. With no choice, I stand there and take it, but I look him in the eye the entire time. If he wants to shoot me, he's going to watch the millions of dollars he would have gotten through our marriage bleed out my brain.

Another heartbeat later, he turns away and goes back to his desk. I don't have to say a word to Rose. We both flee from the room up to my bedroom. I lock the door and drag the heavy armoire in front of it.

Rose is huddled on the other side of the bed, her knees against her chest and her face in the carpet.

Tears are pouring down her cheeks, and mine, I realize as I gather her into my arms and rock her gently against my chest. "I'm so sorry," I whisper. "I was supposed to keep you safe, and he got to you anyway. I never thought he would touch you."

She doesn't respond, and all I can do is hold her until she falls asleep. Then I grab my pillow and blanket off the bed to make her more comfortable.

My brain is strangely empty when I go to my bedside table and pull out both the black card and my cell phone. I dial the number and hit send.

It rings several times, and then a female voice says, "Hello?"

I suck in a slow inhale and blow it out soft enough it's not heard through the line. Then I say, "I'm calling to speak to Adrian, please."

## 6

## VALENTINA

Rose pleads with me again, begging, and it breaks my heart. I slip the gold hoop in my earlobe and close the back, taking a moment to compose myself before we go another round.

"All I'm saying is this is a bad idea," she repeats for the tenth time.

I face her and smooth my hands down the black silk bandage dress that hugs every inch of me a little too tightly. It was Rose's, and she adjusted it for me, despite her reservations about my decision. The dress turns my lack of curves into something enticing for once. I wish I could appreciate it.

My hands are shaking when I answer her. "I get it. But our choices are bad choice A that we've been living with, or bad choice B that is fresh and new and might…"

"Be even worse?" she supplies.

I step into the towering heels, and despite her still grumbling, she kneels at my feet and straps the buckles at my ankle. It is highly likely I'll topple off them and make a fool of myself, but they complete the look. And tonight, I need to look like I mean business. Despite my father thinking I'm useless, I know his world, and I know how things operate. Looking the part is half the battle.

"Do you want to spend another two weeks hiding in here, sneaking out for food when we can't handle being hungry anymore? Because I don't. If we can get rid of Sal, then I'm willing to take the risk. All you have to do is stay here and cover for me. Tell anyone who asks I have my period and there's a mess all over the bathroom. It will gross anyone out enough that they won't ask you for details."

She juts her chin up at me, her eyes glistening. "I just wish you didn't have to make this choice in the first place."

I kneel and capture her chin in my hand. "This is not your fault. You are not to blame in any of this, so get that thought out of your head now."

With a sniff, she nods. "Fine. What else do you need from me?"

I drag her to stand in a hug. "Help me out of the window and pray I don't break my neck in these damn shoes before I can sneak off the grounds."

That earns me a little smile as she helps me steady myself on the way toward the window. The balcony leads out to a fire escape, so it's a matter of squeezing down a narrow flight of stairs to reach the grass below.

It's all too easy to reach the street, order a car, and make it to the casino address the voice on the phone had given me. I didn't know if it had been Adrian himself, as I hadn't spoken to him long enough to memorize his voice, but it is the only lifeline I have.

The casino is packed. People laugh and drink as the sound of slots and bells and crowds press in on me. I squeeze through the throngs of people hunting for the side entrance. I'd heard this special side door was only for those in the society. And only society members can gain access. As I approach, I'm not quite sure if I'm a part of the society or not. I've never participated in any of my father's business dealings, and the party I attended a couple of weeks ago was my first society event. I don't have time to consider it further as a man steps in front of the door, blocking my way.

I barely have time to slap a sultry smile on my red-painted lips before I reach him. "Hi," I say. Smooth. Super smooth.

The man is at least a foot taller than me, his black hair tied back into a ponytail. He narrows his eyes and jerks his thumb toward the gambling crowds. "This isn't a place for little girls. Turn around." His voice holds a hint of an accent that I can't place.

I try to give him something like a cross between sexy and serious. Even as I have to focus on not shivering under the hard edge of his stare. "I'm not a little girl, and I was invited to this party."

His eyes narrow, and he steps toward me. I refuse to back down, thinking of Rose and how much we need to be saved.

"Who invited you then?" His tone says he doesn't believe a word I've said.

I dig into the small clutch I brought that holds my phone, lip gloss, and all the cash Rose and I could scrape together and produce the card. He doesn't even look at it closely before he's holding the door open for me. He presses a black stamp onto my hand and waves me through.

I whisper, "Thank you," as I pass and head down a long hallway. The rug under my feet is a rich crimson, and glittering sconces light the way. The floor tilts downward as I walk, like going down an incline before the carpet ends, and I reach a concrete floor and a barrage of shouting.

In what looks like an open parking garage is a roped-off area. Seats are set up around it on three sides, and two men in the middle are beating on each other with their bare fists. I take a step backward, the light and comfort of the long tunnel looking a little more appealing than this...brawling.

But then I spot him. Adrian. He's on the far side of the ring with two other men flanking him. He's dressed similarly to our previous meeting, except in place of the bow tie, the collar of his black shirt is open, revealing the long line of his throat.

I focus on him now. It seems like the only safe place with blood flying from the beating in the ring. If I think about it, if I look, I'll go to some dark places. Places I've visited courtesy of Sal and the video library he enjoys forcing me to watch.

Like gravity, his gaze hits mine, and I feel it through my entire body, all the way to my sore toes. It's like a balm. A soothing, cooling calm across my senses as we stare at each other. Yes. I felt something like this when we met. Like my entire being knows that in his presence, I'm utterly safe, and for as long as I'm with him, I can relax and let down my guard.

He gestures at one of the men beside him, and that man skirts the ring, the mixed crowd watching the fight parting around him like they fear touching him. Then he's beside me and gently leading me away from the ring toward another hallway. This one is identical to the first, and I let the man grip my elbow gently to tug me beside him. It should occur to me to ask who this man is and why he's taking me away from Adrian, but I don't. It's not like I have a choice in my presence here. I signed away my choice the second I walked into the building.

The man opens a door, tugs me into a room, and then closes the door again, leaving me alone. I stare around the space. It looks like an empty office, maybe. The furniture is deep polished wood, but nothing is on the desk or decorates the walls.

I'm tempted to sink into the leather chair on the far side of the room but decide to stay upright, prepared for anything. Who knows what this man is going to ask for in exchange for his help. But to save Rose, I'm prepared to do anything.

I don't know how long I stand there waiting, but eventually, the doorknob turns, and two men enter, followed closely by Adrian. I meet his eyes until my fear gets the better of me, and I drop my gaze to the floor.

"Well, look at you," he says.

His words make me glance up. The other two men have flanked me, but I don't even care, not when his eyes are trained on me, his gaze raking me from head to toe. I can almost feel it but not in the same creepy way Sal's beady eyes linger on my tits or ass. No, this is different. It feels like he's inspecting me, looking beneath my layers to the parts I keep hidden. Adrian drinks me in, and when he stops, he focuses on my hair. It's tied back into an elegant chignon—done by Rose, of course—but I wanted it restrained.

"Everyone out," he orders. His booming voice startles me, and I jump in my shoes, barely managing to remain standing. The men don't question him. They simply walk around him and close the door once they leave.

I'm alone with him for the first time since the party. Like really truly alone and I'm not sure what to do with myself. My courage is flaking away with every twiddling second we stand here, and I try to hold on to why I've come in the first place. *Rose.* I have to save Rose.

"You came for a reason," he states. It's not a question, so I'm not sure how to answer. I'm not sure what answer will make him help me—help us.

I clear my throat and straighten my shoulders, doing my best to appear strong. "I came to see you."

"For...?" he prompts. The iciness of his tone makes me shiver. "If you can't say it out loud, then you aren't ready to be here, Val."

When he steps forward, I catch the smoky ginger scent of him, and suddenly, I can't focus. Not on anything but how very close he's standing now. Or how his hand reaches behind my head and pulls the pins from the bottom of my hair to release it.

The heft of it tumbles out of its restraints, and he catches it in his hand. I don't know why the idea of his hand in my hair makes me feel so... warm. No, not warm, hot. I've never felt this way around a man. Warm and needy. All the experience I have with sex is visual and forced. I don't know what to do with these developing feelings except lean into his touch and drag his scent deep into my lungs to keep it there, to memorize it.

"Tell me why you're here, Val." His voice is just above a whisper, and I feel the heat of his breath on my ear.

I swallow thickly as reality crashes back down around me. His hand is still sifting through my curls, and I don't dare pull away as I speak. "I need help with a problem."

"What kind of problem?" he asks, his eyes focused on my hair.

If all he wants is to rub my scalp and play with my curls, then I can handle this. I force another ragged breath into my lungs. I'm here, so I might as well commit now.

"I want you to kill my fiancé."

His fingers freeze and snap into a fist, pulling my hair tight against my scalp. Not painfully, but I'm aware of him there, his touch lingering like an invisible noose around my neck. One wrong move, and I'm as good as dead.

"Do you understand what you're asking me for?"

I nod, my courage gone now that I've stated what I want.

He continues moving his fingers again. "And why do you think I can help you with this little problem of yours?"

*Shit.* Do I tell him he's the society's version of a boogeyman? Does a monster already know he's a monster, or will he lash out at the person who informs him?

"Um...well..."

"Val. Just say it. You haven't shied away from being honest with me so far."

His eyes lock on mine, and I let myself relax into his touch, his hand practically cradling my head now. "You have a reputation of being ruthless. My cousin says you're dangerous and scary."

"Yet you are here." Another statement so I don't say anything.

"Do you understand what you're asking me for?" He asks the question once more while his fingers massage the base of my neck. His touch feels so good, I barely stifle a moan of pleasure. "Do you understand there is always a price for these types of things? Normally, it comes in the form of money, guns, drugs, or…" His voice trails off, and then he continues, "Are you willing to pay the price? Any price?"

I nod without thinking. Because there's really nothing to consider. I'll do anything to keep Rose safe, even if it means sacrificing myself.

I meet his eyes and nod again. "I understand."

He untangles his fingers gently and takes a large step away. I lean toward him, craving the touch he just revoked.

"If you understand…then strip. Take everything off and put it on the desk."

# 7

# ADRIAN

*I* don't know if asking her to strip is a test for her or a test for myself. After only two minutes in this woman's presence, I'm already butting up against the edge of my control. And that fucking dress should be outlawed. I want to pluck out every single man's eyeballs who dared to look at her in it or dared to covet her because I watched many of the fight's spectators note her passing.

If I can do this. If I can watch her remove every single scrap of clothing and not take her right here on the desk, then I know I can handle helping her.

My inability to maintain my control isn't something I'm willing to consider yet.

Her hands shake as she lifts them to the thick straps that cut into her shoulders. I notice now that the dress is maybe one size too small for her. No wonder it looks so fucking indecent.

Then as if she forgot what she was doing, she drags her hands over to the curve of her waist. I spot the zipper under her arm and wait for her to ask for my help. Again.

When people ask me for things, it usually pisses me off because I don't work for anyone but myself. But it's not the same with those big eyes staring at me so innocent and full of hope. It also happens that I've been dreaming about ripping Sal's dick off since I met him. Killing him will be no hardship for me.

"Val," I whisper. "If you don't ask for what you need, you'll never get it."

Her eyes flash to mine, locking deep, shooting straight to my cock. I swallow and step into her, taking the top of her zipper between my fingers. "Do you want me to help you?"

She nods once, her fingers shaking as they brush my knuckles to pull away.

I carefully slide the zipper down, ensuring I don't catch it on her skin or any underwear. Underwear she doesn't seem to be wearing. A ridiculous concept since I'm sure by looking at her this woman has never even had an orgasm in her life. Sweet innocence rolls off her in waves. I almost feel like an asshole for wanting to turn her over the desk right now just to show her what she's been missing. Almost.

When I've finished lowering the zipper, I drop my hands. Any closer and I won't be able to keep from touching her. Pushing her further than she can handle right now.

"I don't have all night, sweetie. If you're serious about this, a little nudity isn't a high price to pay. Especially for what you're asking."

She doesn't meet my eyes this time as she speaks. "It's not about being naked. I don't know what you're going to do when I've taken my clothes off. Maybe you'll..."

"Rape you?" I supply.

I tuck my hands into the curls at the nape of her neck. "Sweetie, you're already wet for me. I don't need to rape you to have you. But if it makes you feel better, all I'm going to do is look at you. For now."

"Just look?" she whispers, finally bringing a tear-filled gaze to mine.

I release my hold on her. "Look and maybe touch. Nowhere you'd find objectionable. I promise you."

She stutters out a breath and then quickly jerks the straps of her dress down, down, down to peel off her hips. The tight material has cut into her skin in places, leaving red lines on her creamy pink skin. Her motions are jerky, almost angry, and I smile as she finishes throwing her clothing and shoes on the table.

"Earrings too?" she asked.

I shake my head. "You can leave those. It's fine. But let's be reasonable here. Fold your clothing up and put it on the table like a civilized person."

Her hands shake again, but she does as directed, and my smile grows. Until I finally get a good look at her.

More than just the faint red lines of her dress mar her. Bruises, both old and new, dot her body from her ankle to her neck. I can see the edges under whatever makeup she's applied to cover them.

Rage fires through me, and I must step away and take a moment so I don't walk out of this room, go to her house, and shoot every motherfucker in sight.

What's worse is I hate the fucking way she tucks her delicate chin almost all the way into her chest. As if trying to protect her face without actually making the moves to do it. She can sense my anger but doesn't realize it's not directed toward her.

I circle her another time, allowing my anger to cool slightly. It's not her fault the men in her life don't understand what a good thing they were given. But I can see it. I see her for what she really is. Some part of me rebels at taking her innocence and corrupting it.

Because the moment I touch her, and I will touch her, all that innocence will be mine.

When I come back around to her front, I lean in to force her gaze to mine, but she studiously looks away. No, she is disassociating from this. And I can't have that.

Gently, like cupping a baby bird on the end of my finger, I lift her chin away from her chest until I can see her eyes better. She still refuses to look at me.

"Val, look at me, please." I keep my tone even despite the need to eviscerate and extract revenge for every mark made on her skin.

It takes a few moments of the patience I barely cling to before she meets my eyes. There's nothing but sharp fear there, and I hate it. It's all accusation and hatred, and even though it's not directed at me, I still don't like it.

"I told you I wouldn't hurt you. Breathe, Little Angel, breathe."

Her sob comes out first, and she clutches her hand over her lips, eyes wide. I nod and let her go, let her break down in whatever way she needs so I can be there to put the pieces back together. Even if she hadn't been able to remove her clothing. Even if she walked out of here right now and I never saw her again, I'd still pay a visit to her bastard fiancé and show him what kind of man takes his anger out on his woman. Men like Sal. Men like my father.

I take a moment to compose myself while she does the same. When her hand falls away and she stands with her fingers tucked together behind her back again, I return to meet her eyes. "Now, tell me again what you want me to do to your fiancé?"

She shivers but keeps her gaze on mine. I like a little steel in her spine when it comes to asking for what she wants, and right now, the hard glint in her eyes is making me hard as a fucking rock.

"I want you to kill my fiancé, Sal."

"Any particular way?"

She shakes her head, losing some of the bravado.

I don't think she considered that she'd have options on how it's done. I give her a gentle smile. The ones I use for the society and the simpering girls who will never be strong enough to become my wife.

Then she speaks up before I can question her further. "I want it to hurt. I want him to hurt before he dies."

Fuck, yes. There she is. Not just an angel then...an angel of death. My angel.

I lift her chin again, only an inch because she kept it up this time, staring me down, daring me to ask questions.

"Anything else you need before we discuss payment?"

She blinks and gestures at herself. "This isn't payment?"

"Val. You should know how our world works by now. There's always a cost, and it's often more than you ever wanted to pay to begin with."

I study her as she thinks it through. She came here for a killer, and a killer is what she found. But is she brave enough to see it through? I already know the answer. I'm waiting to see if she does.

After a heartbeat, she nods. "I'll do whatever it takes. I don't have any money, but I can pay you any other way, or once Sal is gone, maybe I'll be engaged to someone else, someone who actually has some..."

The idea of another man touching her hits me so hard I jerk away and spin so she doesn't see the sheer rage on my face at the thought. It would scare her too much, too soon. She's not ready to see that part of me.

"I have more money than I need. We'll make a deal, you and me."

She steps toward me, her bare feet shuffling against the floor. "Then tell me what you want."

Finally, she understands.

I face her again and stare into her deep doe eyes. Fucking hell, she is gorgeous. And a fighter with an innocent soul. A combination I seem to be drawn to.

"Isn't it obvious, Angel? I want you."

"Me?" At that moment, I see the true depths of her naïvety and wonder if she can even make it in this world. I've already decided she's mine, so we'll figure it out together.

"You, Val. From the moment I met you outside that bathroom, I've wanted you. But I'm not Sal. I won't abuse you like he did. When I take you, you'll scream in pleasure and rip into my back with your nails out of sheer bliss. I promise you that."

Her arms tremble as if she's picturing it. The urge to reach down and cup her pussy to see if she is wet overwhelms me. A tiny part of my brain says I promised I wouldn't. I can't scare her away yet. I need to make her mine first.

I back her up against the table, caging her body in with mine without touching any of her soft skin on display. I lean down, my fists beside her hips, and stop only inches from her lush pout. "That's my offer. You gain your freedom from Sal, but you become mine in return. You should know I'm not an easy man. I won't force you to do anything you don't want, but I expect, if you make this choice willingly, that you come to it willingly."

"What's—" she starts again, voice barely above a whisper. "What's that mean?"

"It means when you come to me, and Angel, I can't wait until you do, then you'll be mine in every way. You can tell me when you don't like something or if you disagree, but I won't accept anything less than obedience and your willing participation."

"Obedience?" Another tremor in her tone.

"Get thoughts of him out of your fucking head right now. I said I'm not that shitbag fiancé of yours, and I mean it. You will belong to me, and you'll be treated like the angel you are. I have other means to get my way that don't involve putting bruises on your body."

Her eyes are wide, tears filling the brims. I let my temper out just enough to scare her, but it's already too late. Gathering her into my arms gently, I'm mindful of her bruises and let her weep against my chest.

When she finishes, a dark ring of makeup smudges around her eyes, but she looks up at me and nods. "I understand what you are offering, but I'm not the only person it concerns. I need to talk to my cousin, Rose, first."

"Rose?" I think back to the girl clutching at her friend from the party.

"She's my cousin and my sister and my best friend. I'm doing this for her. If I go, she comes too. We have to decide together."

Gently, I ease her away from me. Grabbing her dress, I kneel at her feet and help her step into it. Her cunt is an inch in front of my face, and my mouth waters to taste her. But I hold back because there will be time soon enough.

Once I zip her into the dress and help her put her shoes back on, she's already wiped her face with a handkerchief. Without the heavy eye makeup, she looks even younger and so fucking corruptible.

I brush my thumb over her cheek and nod. "I'll give you a few days. And then, my angel, you'll come back to me."

# 8

## VALENTINA

*I* don't even have words to describe what I'm feeling as one of Adrian's men leads me out of the office to the casino. We stand in front of the doors, waiting, but I don't realize for what until a black Town Car pulls up in front of me. The man, who doesn't offer his name, opens the door, helps me in, and shuts it behind me.

We pull away, and I try to gather my thoughts. I try to make some semblance of order. If I can give myself to Adrian, our problems are solved. He'll get rid of Sal, and Rose will be safe. The downside is I'd yet again belong to a man. It seems I'm destined to be owned by someone for my entire life. I wouldn't hate the idea if it were the right man.

I think back to the intense look on Adrian's face as he watched me. It was as if he saw every tiny twitch I made and knew exactly why. My face heats, and I press my hands to my cheeks to stifle some of it. He saw the bruises, and now he knows my shame. I don't know if him knowing is better or worse at the moment. It almost feels liberating that someone else knows this secret I've held so long.

The society isn't made of decent people. But...when out in public, mixing with the group, they are meant to look decent. This means the abuse, the rape, the crime, all of it is hidden discreetly away, waiting for business meetings and private affairs. I didn't know much, but I'd seen Rose's and my abuse overlooked constantly. It's always easier to look away than speak up. But only for the witnesses, never for those suffering.

I stare out the window and watch the casino lights fade away. My mind is still on Adrian. Rose is terrified of him. He's supposedly one of the most ruthless men in the society. My father hates him but also won't speak about him because of some feud, so I didn't know much on that side. I prefer not to talk to Sal directly unless my father forces me to spend time with him, so I couldn't get information there either. From my own interactions with him…I'm torn.

I want to rub myself against him and that maddening spicy ginger scent of his. But at the same time, I can see the darkness in his eyes, and I know he's not gentle with everyone he meets. I don't know if it makes me feel better or worse that he's treated me so.

I direct the car to pull up down from the property, and thankfully, he doesn't argue with me about it. As I climb out, I give him a bright smile as if I do this every day. Then I stand on the side of the road until he finally pulls away.

Now I just need to get back into the house without anyone seeing me. Rose is supposed to keep watch for me, but if she's running interference, then I'll have to fend for myself. I take off my shoes this time, determined not to break an ankle, and reach my bedroom window easily. It's dark inside, but the window slides up easily and silently, allowing me to not-so-gracefully climb over the ledge and into my bedroom.

I don't make it even a step before something catches my hair and levers me back. At first, I think it's the window, that my unruly mess of a head got stuck on it somehow, but then the darkness lifts enough for me to see Sal standing right inside, lying in wait for me.

I hit the floor next, barely getting my hands under me to break the fall. Pain shoots up my right arm and into my elbow, but I don't have time to consider it. I scramble forward, intent to get my feet under me and escape, but I don't get far. His heavy boot connects with my ribs, and I lift up enough with the force of the strike to fall back down hard. More pain. Every inhale now hurts, and I cough a few times, ragged and wet. That can't be good.

Sal crouches beside me, his boot almost at eye level, and captures my hand in his. It yanks me off balance, and my shoulder rubs hard across the hardwood.

"I see we've been busy tonight," he spits at me.

I peer up at him and see his eyes locked on the black stamp smudged across the back of my hand.

I want to yank my hand from his grip, but he'll only hurt me worse for fighting back, so I stay still. He wants me to give him a reason to hit me, so I turn my eyes on the floor, even as tears begin to fall against my will.

"You've got nothing to say for yourself, you fucking whore?"

I want to defend myself, but can I really? I'd stripped naked for a stranger as a down payment to kill my fiancé. Not something I can exactly use in my defense. It doesn't matter, though, because he doesn't want me to say anything. Again, he wants any excuse to hurt me, and talking will only give him more opportunities.

I let out another gurgling cough and taste blood in my mouth. Shit. Rose and my Dr. Google medical tips were likely going to have a tough time with internal bleeding. Not like I can throw an Ace bandage on it and call it a day.

Sal's grip digs in tighter as he pulls my hand up to his face. Then he licks the ink there, his tongue wet and hot and thoroughly disgusting. I barely keep my face neutral as bile rushes up my throat. Puking on him will not help the situation.

I study the floor and the tiny droplets of my blood splattered underneath me. Blood dripped out of my mouth, and I hadn't even realized.

Hm. Interesting.

It's okay, though, because I feel myself sliding into that sleepy place. A little pocket of the world where I can go when Sal beats on me. A place to feel nothing until the brutality stops, and I can pick up the pieces that are left. Or Rose can.

It hits me that with him here, I haven't seen her. She should be here waiting for me. I can't ask him because drawing attention to her might make things worse, but my worry slips underneath the calm I'd been building enough to fracture it. If something happens to her, then he'll have finally broken me.

I'm dragged to my feet, his arms around my waist, but I can't stand. The pain from his grip around my ribs is too much. My vision swims in and out of focus, and while he screams, spit flying in my face, all I can think about is Rose and that I hope she stays hidden, safe.

And I hope she doesn't see what's left of me when Sal finishes this. I can see it in his eyes that he wants to kill me. He wants to watch the life leave my eyes just like he watches in those videos of his.

He drags me over to my bed and throws me on top of it. The icy glint of fear is still keeping me from that safe little room in my mind. If I could just see that Rose is okay, then I can lie here and bear whatever he does to my body. As long as she's safe.

He rips off my dress, leaving me naked and exposed to the chilled night air coming in from the open window. If any of the outside guards hear anything, they certainly aren't running to help. In fact, everything seems eerily quiet, apart from his screaming at me about being a whore to Adrian.

Some of his words filter in, and I make the mistake of meeting his eyes.

"There she is," he whispers. "Don't worry, baby. I'm going to treat you so much better than he did. If you weren't waiting for marriage anymore, you should have come to me first. I'm your fucking fiancé."

I can't even open my mouth to refute him. Nothing comes out but a wheezing cough. Then one word. "Rose?"

His face splits into a grin. A sadistic, demented shit-eating grin that chills every inch of me. No.

I glance around, fighting him now, trying to get up, but he shoves me down harder.

Then I see silky dark hair in a light cast by the open door out to the hallway. But I can't see her face.

I sob, ragged and loud in the silence that I'd filled in my head before. I try to wrench from Sal's grip, try to crawl to her, and he lets me, and I don't fucking care because it gets me closer to her.

When I reach her, I dig my fingers into her wrist, checking for a pulse. It's there, barely but there. It takes all my strength to get closer to her and pull her onto my lap.

But I barely graze my hand over her head to move her hair back when Sal has me by the arms again. He jerks me out from under her shoulders, his hands fisted in my hair as he yanks me behind him. I spin, trying to get free to get back to her, to help her, to save her, but he is stronger than me. Soon, he has me up on the bed, his clothed weight pressing me into the mattress as he ties me to the frame. The ropes dig into my skin as I flail and struggle, screaming for Rose. After a moment, he shoves a wad of something in my mouth and tapes over it with duct tape. I stare at him wide-eyed as I realize his erection is pressing into my thigh.

The bastard likes this. He gets off on it. I'd seen it hundreds of times, but now, the proof humping my inner thigh sends bile up my throat again. I have to swallow against it because if I puke now, I'll drown. I can't save Rose if I'm dead.

He doesn't stay long. Once secure, he climbs off the bed and removes his clothing as he stands over Rose.

I want to squeeze my eyes shut because I know what he's going to do to her. Worse, he's going to make me watch it, unable to help her this time. I sob, tears wetting my cheeks. No. He can't take her from me.

Once nude, he rolls her over onto the hardwood. Her hands slap hard against it, and I have one shining moment of relief that she's unconscious and won't be awake for this humiliation.

Then he's on her, pumping into her hard, fast, furiously. I fight against the bonds, my fingers going numb as I try to wrench my wrists free. I scream and scream and scream, trying to get someone to hear me.

But no one comes.

And when he's finished with her, I'm still and silent on the bed watching her red blood, so bright in the hallway light, drip off the end of a knife.

My Rose is gone.

I feel nothing. I am nothing.

The bastard has finally broken me.

When his face breaks my vision, his eyes glassy with adrenaline, I don't even shrink back.

He whispers in my ear, "I'm going to leave you two here for a bit. Let you say your goodbyes. And when your father comes home in a few days, she'll be out of my way, out of his hair, and you're going to tell him she met someone and ran off. If you don't...well...I'll kill everyone you love. And then, once we're married..." He trails the bloody knife down my chest, between my bare breasts. "Well, I'll do the same to you."

Then he's gone, and all I see are Rose's dead eyes. He doesn't realize I have nothing left to lose now. He's already taken the only thing I love from me.

I smile to myself and stop fighting the pain.

I have nothing left to lose.

## 9

## ADRIAN

If I snap at everyone a little more throughout the next week, well, they can fuck off. Even my five give me a wide berth as I go about my business. The only one brave enough to talk to me is Kai, and he keeps things to the point. Until I drop my coffee mug all over the table in my distraction.

"What's up? Your mood wouldn't have anything to do with that Novak girl coming to the fight the other night, would it?"

I scowl at the fine weave of his suit, trying to identify it like I always do, but again, I'm distracted. All I see in my head when I close my eyes is her. The soft fall of her hair as it sifts through my fingers, the cupid bow of her full lips begging for a proper kiss. Hell, the scent of her and how her entire body went rigid when I dropped to my knees to help her dress. Of course, now, after expecting her to show up the following morning, she's nowhere in sight.

"Can I help with something?" Kai offers. It's only because he doesn't push me that I answer him this time.

"What is Novak up to?"

Kai shakes his head, uncertain, a place he definitely doesn't like to be. "You mean Ms. N—"

"Not fucking Val." Although now that he mentions it, I do want to know why she isn't currently in my bed naked and sleeping off an orgasm. But I don't tell him that. "No, her father. He's been out of town for a while. His business trips don't usually last so long, and when they do, he takes Sal with him. I want to know where he's been, what Sal has been up to in his absence, and where Valentina is at all times."

Kai nods, clearly relieved to be given a task in his purview, and heads out of the dining room. I should eat something, but I can't focus. Even more so now that I have spilled coffee all over the place and need to change.

I'm forced to put up a mental barrier to Val and the disruption of her in order to focus. As soon as she's here, and she's mine, I'll be able to relax. Until then, everything reminds me of her and the fact that I don't have her here with me, safe and sound.

Once I'm cleaned up, I head down to the command center, a large room my trusted lieutenants like to use to debrief or prep for something. It's a big enough space to hold us all and doesn't feel as formal as the dining room or living rooms.

Vincent, my first lieutenant, second only in rank to Kai, has his big feet slung up on the desk, his blond ringlets mussed, his white button-down straining against his solid frame. I shove his legs off the table when I come around it and take a seat between him and my fourth lieutenant. Alexei is dressed up today in a suit and tie, which isn't his usual uniform.

"Kai have you on recon today?" I ask Alexei, even while glaring back at Vincent, who's grumbling at me.

"Yeah. Kai is sending me to monitor your little princess."

I shove him out of the chair before he can react and spin away from my grip. "She's not a fucking princess. And when she does come here, you'll be the perfect gentleman."

"But what about you, boss? Are you going to be the perfect gentleman?" he says, backing toward the door.

I stand, my hands crushing the leather of the chair I'd been sitting in. "Let's be very clear. If anyone touches her or so much as looks at Valentina, I will kill him."

The room is deadly silent as I continue. "You may be the people I trust most in the world, but she will be my wife. She just doesn't know it yet."

Both men stare at me with their hands up in an attempt to calm me. I feel foolish. Snapping at my men is not something I usually do. I've seen how easily a man can tear down his entire world by treating his men poorly.

Alexei rushes out before I have time to come up with some kind of an explanation. I won't apologize, but he deserves to know me snapping at him was more about me than him.

That leaves Vincent. I glance over at him, resuming my seat, and stare up at the oversized monitor on the wall. It keeps track of any current operations in my range. But today, it's blank, nothing but a news show on mute with the subtitles scrolling at the bottom.

"You okay, boss?" Vincent finally dares to ask.

"I'm sure Kai has already briefed you. I'm waiting on something, and you know how much I love to be kept waiting."

He snorts his agreement and shifts in his chair to snag his phone off the table. "It's Kai. He's on the fiancé and says he's acting stranger than usual."

I consider this new information. With Val's father out of town, that leaves Sal alone with her and her friend she mentioned...Rosa, Rose... What would make him start acting erratically?

It bothers me, a low thrum in my gut, that I feel like I'm missing a key part of this puzzle. And once I find that missing piece, I'll regret slipping it into the slot to see the entire picture. It doesn't matter, leaving it unfinished isn't an option.

"Go, follow him, let Kai figure out what the elder Novak is up to. If you get anything weird, send me a text so I know immediately."

Vincent scoops up his keys, pockets his phone, and leaves the room without another word. Something I like about the man.

I trust my men, but the itch to have her here under my own gaze is too much, so I try to focus on other things. An upcoming job we were hired to facilitate that should go off without a hitch. Even with Kai at the helm, as he usually is since my father's death, there shouldn't be any problems. So why do I still feel so off?

I resolve to stop being so fucking pussy whipped, especially since I haven't even had her yet, and get back to work. It's not until Kai throws a file folder on the table in front of me later in the day that I realize I'd finally managed to focus and get some shit done.

"What's this?" I ask, already opening the brown kraft folder to peruse the contents.

"It's the surveillance I ordered on Novak. He's in New York. He has been for over a week maybe? There wasn't any definitive answer on when he left. And my spy on the inside of Novak's place was MIA when I tried to contact him."

I shove the maps I'd been working on to the side and bring the file flat onto the glossy surface. While thinking, I slip out of my jacket, roll up my sleeves, and settle back into the chair. Novak is working on an oceanic smuggling deal. The idea looks lucrative with very little oversight from law enforcement if they've already lined up a ship and forged customs documents.

Knowing this stuff about my enemy always helps inform my next move, yet I'm annoyed there isn't one mention of Valentina.

"What about the girl?" I ask, still scanning the images he provided.

Kai shakes his head. "She hasn't left the house in days from what I can tell and was last seen on the night she came to the casino. Maybe she decided to hide out since her father is gone and her creepy fiancé is lurking around."

"Why is Sal around? Doesn't he usually go with Novak on these trips? What's he been doing all this time while Novak has been gone?"

Finally, Kai takes the seat beside me and settles in to talk. "From what I can tell, he's been beating on prostitutes and spending Novak's money right under his nose. Mostly on the prostitutes and then to their pimps to keep them from bashing his head in. It helps his family has a solid foothold in that industry."

If an industry is what you could call it. I always preferred the term human trafficking for what Sal and his family get wrapped up in. While I have no problem putting a bullet in someone's ear, I draw the line with hurting women and children like that.

A vision of my mother's face flashes in my mind for a heartbeat before I shake it away and look back over Kai's report. "Get Vincent back here. He hasn't texted me, and I want to know more about what this jackhole has been up to since his babysitter has been gone. And for fuck's sake, find out where Val is."

"She's at the house, boss," he supplies. "I've had people on it since we took her home the other night. She hasn't left the place once. Why does she need to with the size of her staff?"

With Sal out doing whatever the fuck knows what, and Novak in New York seemingly indefinitely, this might be the only shot I get. I check my watch and then the window. The sun will be going down soon. Perfect.

"Round up the team. We're going in to get her." The minute the words are out of my mouth, I know they are the right move. I can feel it under my skin, urging me to find her, take her, touch her.

"What are you thinking?" Kai asks, not even pretending to move on my orders.

I drag him up by his very expensive suit collar. "We're going after her, and once she's here, I can stop thinking about her and actually get some work done."

It takes Kai another minute to follow me. Of all my men, he's often the only one who will disagree with me on things. Something I've always appreciated about him.

"Are you sure about this? If Novak finds out it was you who took his daughter, he'll declare war."

"Aren't we already at war? And we both know he doesn't give a shit about her unless it's to use her in a bargain. It's the only reason Sal is in her life to begin with."

With no further argument, he rounds up the rest of the team until all seven of us are standing on the driveway waiting for the cars to take us. Technically, I could have done this alone or with Kai, but I want to be prepared for any strange security Sal might have put into place during Novak's absence. Without our usual spy, our intel is too old to risk going in alone.

I feel better on the drive to the house. But then as we pull up to the gate, my stomach drops out. The entire house is dark, and it looks deserted. Even on lower staff days, the lights would all be turned on, security would be monitoring the gate, and hell, even a chubby guard dog was known to roam the property on occasion. But now, there's nothing but eerie quiet, which settles unevenly across my shoulders.

If something has happened to her, then Sal is the next person who will get a visit tonight. I don't care if he helped or not.

We pull up down the road and hoof it to the gate, Andrea pulling up last since she can work the charm on the mostly male staff if necessary.

Even the sounds of the woods around the property feels quiet. We enter through a servant's side door, the one the staff usually take, and find the entire place empty. Everything is shiny and clean. It's like someone told the staff to take a few days off and not return.

It doesn't bode well. I palm my handgun and lead the way through the kitchen and down the hall. It's not far to her bedroom, according to the earlier spy's maps, but it's not the darkness that makes me stop in the middle of the corridor. It's the acrid scent of death in the air.

A scent I'll never forget.

## 10

## VALENTINA

*I* don't know how long I lay there. More than hours, but less than weeks maybe? The time doesn't seem to have any meaning or form. It doesn't matter because I can't feel anything, not in this place I've gone in my mind. The place where nothing happened and I'm asleep, comfortable in my bed, instead of tied down like an animal.

I might be able to convince myself if my stench wasn't so strong. It's not just unwashed skin, but I know I've made a mess of my bed, of the floor no doubt, and no one dared to do anything to help me. I'd always gotten along well with the servants, treating them like family and giving them gifts during the holidays. It would seem that friendliness had always been an illusion. Not a single one of them would risk untying me. Only the maid ventured in far enough to give me a few sips of water the first day he'd left me here. Then she took one look at…she took one look at everything and never returned.

I've rubbed the skin on my wrists raw from trying to loosen the ties, but Sal has had enough practice at securing prisoners. The knots won't budge.

Rose would help me. She'd risk anything to help me. Something flashes in my mind, a vision of Rose's eyes, but they don't look right, and I shove the image away for fear of it taking hold and staying in my head. Rose doesn't look like that. She's beautiful and vibrant and will help me as soon as she can.

I drift in and out of consciousness, not sure where the nightmares end and reality begins. Everything hurts. It hurts to breathe or move. I've lost most of the feeling in my hands and feet, but I still try to focus on loosening the bonds. It's nothing but pins and stabbing pain with every shift. Rose wouldn't give up, so I can't either.

The next time I wake up, the scent in the room is more pungent. I can't breathe through my nose, and when I breathe through my mouth, it makes me gag. So I take shallow breaths and watch the light through the window. It fades to nothing until the room is dark and shadows play across the walls. I've never been afraid of the dark. Why should I be when the monsters walk around in the daylight?

Each pulse of pain through my body is starting to drift off to a hazy end. A few more and maybe I'll fall back asleep for a while. If I sleep, then maybe someone will untie me before I wake up again. Maybe Rose will be here with me when I wake up again. It's the only solace I can find as my body starts to give out inch by inch.

When I open my eyes again, I can barely pull my eyelids apart. Good, why should I anyway? Not when everything hurts, and I can't breathe right through the smell. But something new happens when I slit my eyes open this time. Someone is leaning over me.

I should be scared, right? Did Sal come back to finish killing me like he promised? Maybe he decided to forget the money my wedding will bring in, in favor of killing me slowly and painfully.

I try to say something to the face. It's not Sal, nor any servant in the house. But I know his face. He's familiar to me, yet I can't think of where or how I know him. His hair looks shiny in the light. The overhead light is now on, I realize slowly.

His mouth is moving. It's a pretty mouth, full and made for kissing. I don't know anything about kissing except for what Sal has forced on me. If Sal knew I thought about kissing this stranger, he'd definitely kill me.

I drift again. Hands are on me, and I want to fight them off, slap them away, like Rose would do, but I don't have the strength. I let them touch me and can't even open my eyes to look at them.

The next time I inch my eyes open, there's something wet on them. Was I crying? I thought I'd run out of tears days ago, weeks ago, years ago.

Someone is speaking to me, soothing and low, as a pressure gently taps against my shoulders. It takes me a long time to figure out that the voice doesn't want me to get up. I lift my hand high, and it flops back to the bed because I'm not tied up anymore. My limbs are still pins and needles punctuated with pain, but I can move them again, so that's a good sign. Maybe my father came home and saw what Sal did to me. Is it sad that a daughter thinks her father will save her even after years of neglect?

"Stay the fuck down, Val," a voice says. No one calls me Val. I blink against the bright light of the room, and then suddenly, it's not as bright. The voice dimmed the lighting so I can open my eyes fully.

I blink a few more times and stare up into the face I thought I remembered from a dream. "Where am I?"

A warm sensation slides down my arm, and I glance over to watch him run a cloth on the same path. "What are you doing?"

"I'll answer your questions if you stop struggling to get up," he says.

I immediately like his voice. It's deep and full of authority and power, but not edged with cruelty like Sal or my father. He makes me want to please him, so I stay still and let him work. Unconsciousness is still hovering at the back of my mind, ready to drag me under again. I know I'm not strong and that I need to rest, but I can't while he's there with that face and that voice and those lips. "I like the way you sound," I grate out. My own voice is scratchy and raw.

From the screaming. I screamed for a long time, but no one ever came to help me.

"Don't speak, Angel. You need to rest your throat. I'm bathing you since it gives me pleasure and calms me down, and because I want you healthy again. As for where you are, you're in my home, but I've told you this several times, and it keeps slipping your mind. Don't worry, though. The doctor says it's normal, and you should start recovering soon."

I shake my head, and he tsks at me, so I go still again. "Doctor? I don't remember a doctor either."

Things are starting to spin, and I let my eyes drift close. "Rest, Val. I've got you. No one is going to hurt you ever again."

And because he says it in that voice, I believe him enough to relax and let myself drift again.

Things seem brighter the next time I wake. I open my eyes and stare up at a white ceiling. The fabric under my hands is soft and lush and smells faintly like ginger. It comes back in a rush, except now, I remember the man speaking to me had been Adrian. Although, I can't remember how I got to his house, or in his bed, or—I lift the covers gently and stare underneath— in his clothes?

I let myself believe, maybe, I really am safe as I drift off again. This time, it's not nightmares clawing their way through my mind; it's a voice, a strong, authoritative voice, telling me to rest and come back to him.

## 11

## ADRIAN

*I* stare down at the little man who has served my men and me for years, and it's the first time I want to crush his little skull. It's not his fault I'm on edge, nor is it his fault Valentina hasn't woken completely despite the week of round-the-clock care he's provided.

"Doctor, if you tell me some gibberish about the body and healing one more time, then I'm going to rethink my no-guns-in-the-bedroom rule. Tell me what to do in order to help her heal enough to be conscious. She's been in and out of it for a week, and I'm concerned about her memory. She doesn't seem to remember much of what happened to her, me saving her, or even the fact we've met before."

To his credit, the doctor doesn't quake under his wire-rimmed glasses, despite my tone eliciting that reaction in greater men than him. "Mr. Doubeck, as I explained before, Ms. Novak was dehydrated, malnourished, and fighting off infections from her various injuries. These things take time and antibiotics to heal. Once she is stronger, I'll add in a steroid, which will assist in her healing process. You must be patient."

"And her memory?" I prompted. "What do you say about that?"

"We can get her a CT scan when she can move around on her own. For now, she has no injury to the head that I can tell. What she is going through is likely a reaction to her trauma. I suggest consistency and being gentle with her as she recovers. Can you do that?"

I swallowed the biting reply I queued up. I didn't like his challenge to me, but I appreciated the ferocity for which he defended her. "Don't let her die, Doctor, or others will follow immediately afterward."

He turned back toward my bedroom, where she'd been recovering since I brought her here, and marched straight to her bedside. It grated on my nerves as he adjusted her IV, checked her vital signs, and then inspected her injuries. When I found her, most of her body was covered in bruises and blood. He'd beat her and then bound her naked to her own bed. I feared blinking or else I'd see her like that again. When I'd walked into the room, I saw the dead woman on the floor, her friend Rose, I guessed, and assumed the worst had happened. But when I'd checked her pulse and felt the faint flutter of her heartbeat, I knew she was so much stronger than she looked.

If anyone decides to test her strength again, they'll find me answering the challenge instead of her. I only prayed we found Sal before I had to go out there and hunt him down myself.

When the doctor completed his exam, he turned to face me again. "She's mending, Mr. Doubeck. Be patient and be gentle with her. That's what she needs right now."

Not trusting myself not to say something cutting, I gave him a curt nod and jerked my head toward the door. He didn't need time to get the hint. The doctor fled, and I approached the bedside to look her over.

The bruises I could see above the covers were changing shade, something I knew to be a good thing from my fighting days. The IVs were helping ensure she received enough nutrition, but I needed her to wake up so I could stuff her full of her favorite foods and put some curves on her too lean frame.

The door opens as I am about to get some water to give her another sponge bath. Kai entered, his frustration evident by the fact he'd taken his jacket off, and his tie hung loose around his neck. "What is it?"

He scowls as he glances over my shoulder at Valentina. I move into his line of sight so he can't look at her. I don't want anyone looking at her while she is weak and unable to defend herself properly. Until then, I'll be here to protect her.

"The fucker has gone to ground. He hasn't been back to his apartment, hasn't been to the Novak house, and he hasn't been to his usual sleazeball haunts. I don't know where he is, and I'm about to start razing each of the disgusting establishments he manages to the ground to root him out."

I shrug. "Did you come here for my permission? I said find him, and I don't care how you do it."

It's not just the hunt that has him frustrated then. "What else?"

"Her father is still in New York, and he hasn't even made a move to come home. It's like he has no idea his daughter almost died or that his niece is dead."

I waved at where Val lay unconscious. "You think he's going to advertise his handiwork to her father? Not if he thinks he can still marry her and get access to her money."

The thought makes me want to kill him all over again. Slowly. Painfully. I want to inflict every injury he did on her and then see how long he can stay alive, left bound to a bed, alone, with no food, water, or medical care. I suspect a lot less time than she did.

"When Sal surfaces, let me know immediately, especially if you get a hold of him. Keep me updated on the movements of her father and note if he makes any sudden changes like he knows what happened here."

Kai nods. "Anything else?"

I've already turned back to the bed, my attention on the way her chest rises and falls. "Keep one of the five on the door at all times and have Andrea go get some clothes for her. She's going to wake up soon, and she'll need something to wear."

He doesn't need to say anything. I hear the soft settle of the door against the frame to indicate he left the room.

I was going to bathe her, but right now, after talking to the doctor and then Kai, I need to calm down. So I sit in the chair next to her bed and watch her carefully. Each little blip on the machines monitoring her condition signals she's still with me, but it's also a reminder that I could have lost her before I even made her mine. I won't make that mistake again. The second she is well enough, I'll be sure she knows she belongs to me in every way.

I don't know how long I sit with her. Long enough that Andrea returns with two large white paper bags. "She isn't my size, so I went out and got some things that will fit. And things she can wear as her injuries heal."

I can't believe I didn't consider she'd need comfortable clothing to wear until she was back to full strength. Once again, I'm reminded why my team is the best.

She sets the bags at the end of the bed and does a quick once-over of the equipment and me. "Do you need anything else, boss? Want me to sit with her while you get some rest?"

"I'm not leaving her. I'll rest when she is conscious again."

"Any word?"

"The doctor continues to tell me I must wait. Little does he know I'm not a very patient man."

She snorts. "He knows just fine. He's the one who had to stitch up a bullet wound twice when you didn't wait for it to heal before you went back to work."

"Well, he gets paid well enough. Two rounds of stitches are nothing." I know she's trying to take my mind off worrying about Valentina, but it's not working.

"You can go now. Make sure you guys rotate shifts on the door. No one comes in except one of you, me, or the doctor."

She gives me a salute and leaves as quietly as she entered. I turn my attention back to Val and shift my chair closer. When she wakes up, I want to be ready to reassure her that she's safe. Every time she's woken since I found her, she's been groggy and barely discernible. And each and every time, I add one more mental tally to what I'm going to take out of Sal's hide in payback. As of right now, nothing will be left when I'm finished with him.

I take her hand in mine. It's bruised across the knuckles from where she fought back. Her nails are jagged and split, but worst of all is the raw skin around her wrists from trying to free herself from her bindings. She never stopped fighting, even as her body began to give out under the strain of captivity. I'm so proud of her.

Gently, I smooth my thumb over a pale patch of healthy skin on the back of her hand. The need to touch her is overwhelming, but I won't hurt her, not like he did.

Her fingers twitch against the plush duvet, and I lift my hand to make sure she doesn't move and cause me to touch one of her wounds. When her hand curls into a fist, I scan up her arm and into her face. It's drawn tight, like she is having a nightmare, so I ease out of my seat and gently prod her shoulder. "Val, wake up, Val. You're dreaming."

To my surprise, her eyes fly open, and she lets out a gasp. Then she settles back on the bed and looks at me with full wide eyes, and says, "Rose?"

## 12

## VALENTINA

*I*'m not sure how long it takes me to realize I'm awake. It takes a few blinks to clear my hazy vision and then notice the strange ceiling. Then down to the unfamiliar bedding and the bandages around my wrists.

A figure looms at the side of the bed, and I simply react, clawing out while trying to scramble away. I don't know why, but something inside me needs to hide.

"Stop fucking moving," a deep voice says. It soothes something in me that had raised its hand, prepared to strike. Now, it paces, waiting to see if we're safe.

"Who? What's going on?" I'm still baring my nails at the figure when the light flicks on. I stare at the figure and recognize him. "Adrian?"

He plops on the edge of the bed, grabs my shoulders in his huge hands, and gently eases me back onto the mound of pillows. I let him guide me since I have no choice.

"Who the fuck else would be sitting beside his own damn bed?" he grouses while he adjusts the covers around me again, then checks the line on my IV. I trace the path of it to the back of my hand. Then his words filter through some of the haze.

Own? Bed? I clutch the covers and drag them up to my chest. I'm wearing someone's black dress shirt, but still... "What's going on? Why am I here?"

For a moment, I fear he won't answer me since he won't even look at me. Not that I'm eager to put myself under his intense gaze. When he finally does shift those dark eyes to mine, I flinch. Oh yeah, I forgot just how heavy the weight of his regard is.

"Tell me what you remember," he says. It's nothing short of an order. The tiny part of me that wants to rebel against a man giving me orders doesn't stir. I want to please him, the same way I have since I met him.

I clear my throat, only now realizing how dry and scratchy it feels. So I whisper because he's looking at me like he won't wait forever. "I came to see you. Rose was covering the house so I could sneak out. I asked you to..." It comes back in a flash—me asking him to kill Sal and him making the offer under the condition of well...me. A hot flush hits my neck and cheeks. I can't believe I stripped naked for him or, worse, that I liked it.

He gently tilts my chin up to force our gazes together again. "Asked me to?"

"Kill my fiancé," I whisper.

The very corner of his lips tilts up, and I can't not look at them. It's as if that tiny corner is proof I gave him what he wants, and for some reason, I want more of that tiny smile, more of a smile period. I want him to look at me like he did at the party that first time we met. I know I shouldn't, not while I'm engaged to Sal, but he was never my choice.

I'm still staring at his lips when he asks his next question. "What else do you remember?"

Everything in my head feels hazy. Like a dream. "Not much. We spoke, and I went home, but after that, I can't remember anything until I woke up just now."

"Nothing?"

Something in his voice worries me. Obviously, I should be able to remember something else than what I've told him. Or why bother questioning me. "Why are you asking? What else am I supposed to remember?"

I scan his face, waiting for a sign of what he's looking for. After years in my house under my father and then Sal, I've gotten very good at reading people's every twitch. Sometimes it was the only thing between me and Sal cornering me in a hallway and leaving bruises on my skin as punishment for being unable to touch me the way he wants.

He stands with his back to me, but I can't help but notice the rigid line of his spine and the hard set of his shoulders. He's angry, and I don't know why.

"Tell me what I should remember, and I can try. Let me try, please." I don't know why I'm begging him, but something inside me is telling me he might be my only chance at safety. I can't lose it.

His hands clench along his thighs, and I shrink back into the pillows. I know how my father's hands feel on me and how Sal's hands feel on me. So far, Adrian hasn't hurt me, so I don't know what to brace for or what to expect when he strikes out.

When his arm flies out, I clench up, turning my face away to protect it. The sound of glass breaking makes me flinch more, and I huddle into the pillows, trying to use the covers as some kind of meager protection.

When everything is quiet, I slowly blink my eyes open and risk a glance toward him. He's standing at the side of the bed, his eyes angry, his mouth set in a grim line. When he speaks, his tone is soft and gentle. "Look at you. Why are you cowering away from me?"

I whisper immediately. "You're angry."

"So?"

"I just...don't want to get hit anymore." I know I sound defeated, and I hate the thread of it in my voice, especially in front of him.

He sinks slowly onto the bed, his hips almost against my knees. "I don't fucking hit women, Val. And I would never ever hurt you."

I assimilate that information. My father never pretended he was a good man. Lord knows Sal prided himself on the way he overpowered and demeaned women. Adrian telling me he won't hurt me makes me want to believe him so badly my chest aches.

"I don't know you. You're the last person I saw, and now I'm here, in your bed, hooked up to hospital equipment. What am I supposed to think?"

His eyes go wide. "You think I could have done this to you? You asked me why I'm angry; it's because I found you like this. I'm angry for you, not at you."

Is there a difference when it comes to men's anger? It really doesn't matter. I stretch out and throw back the covers to reveal my bare legs. My yellow and purple bruised bare legs. I can't look at them, so I don't. It's not something I can help right now.

"What are you doing?" He reaches out but then stops so he doesn't touch any of my numerous injuries.

"I'm assuming by how upset you are that Sal isn't dead. He's the only one, besides my father, who inflicts this much damage on my body. If he's not dead, then I need to go home or else he'll come searching for me, and the next time he gets his hands on me, things will be worse."

He gestures at me in one sweep of his big hand. "Worse than this?"

I shrug and focus on shifting my weight to the edge of the bed. But I don't even make it an inch before he's gently curving his hands around my shoulders again and shoving me back into the nest of pillows.

"You can't leave yet. You aren't well, and if you try to stand right now, you'll likely pass out and ruin the work my doctor has done to keep you alive. Besides..." He stiffens, his shoulders sinking back. "We made a deal, remember? I hold everyone to the deals they make with me. No exceptions."

His tone is no longer gentle. He's back to the man I met at the party. Command, control, and all the deep dominion men like him cultivate by breathing. I drag the smoky scent of him into my lungs and let it soothe the fear I'd start to let take over. But it's a dream, a fantasy. We made a deal, and here I am, half-dead in his bed. Obviously, thinking someone else could save me had been a mistake.

"Even if Sal doesn't come looking for me, my father will. How will you protect me from him? How can you protect Rose?" Oh, God, Rose. How am I such a shitty friend that I didn't ask about her first?

He tilts his head, the hint of a grin returning. "I have a no-guns-in-the-bedroom rule, Angel, but I promise, I'm fully capable of keeping you safe. Besides, neither Sal nor your father is at your house. Rest now."

The way he says it is so confident, so full of cockiness. I...still want to believe him, despite the bandages, the bruises, and the IV hanging over my head.

"You're scared. I told you to rest, Angel. If you don't make an effort, I'll have the doctor sedate you."

It's not a question, so I don't respond, keeping my eyes somewhere around his left shoulder.

I'm not surprised when he reaches out and guides my chin to look at him again. "You're scared, but you don't have to be. When I let you leave that night, I was stupid enough to think you'd be safe until I did the job you asked of me. That was my mistake, and I'll spend the rest of my life making it up to you. But when I say I can keep you safe, I need you to listen and believe me."

God, I want to. It would be so easy to take his word for it and let him be my shield to the world. I want to believe him so badly that tears slide down my cheeks in frustration. "I don't know if I can believe that because I don't know what safe feels like."

He slides closer on the bed until his legs brush against mine. Like he can't resist touching me, and even though he must, he'll be sure not to hurt me, even then. I look at him this time and watch his face as he speaks.

"We made a deal, and I have every intention of holding up my end of the bargain. Just as you will hold up yours. It's as simple as that. You belong to me, in every way, and I promise you"—his voice takes on a deeper tone, a hint of threat under the bass—"no one will be able to get to you with me in the way."

This time, I do believe him, and the relief makes me dizzy, causing my breathing to come out in short pants. I relax into the pillows for the first time since I woke up. He gently reaches out and takes my hand, his fingers brushing a patch of skin that isn't discolored from bruises.

I'd forgotten how beautiful he is. Not traditionally beautiful like a model or an athlete, but he's big, so much bigger than me. His shoulders must be at least twice as wide. His hands even dwarf mine in his own. I'd forgotten a lot of things about him and how much I liked all of them. I've never risked this feeling before, or else it might get him killed. I don't think Adrian will be that easy to take down.

"So what now?" I ask.

He looks like he's waiting for something, and then it hits me. If I'm here, and he's keeping me safe, then I need to hold up my end of our deal. By the way he'd asked me to strip for him at the casino, I assume he wants more than pithy conversation and a mean Spades partner. I shove the covers farther away from my legs, and he frowns at them, staring between the plush linens and my bare limbs.

When I don't move to climb off the bed, he seems to settle, my hand still tucked into his.

Then slowly, as fear and something else skitters up my spine, I raise my knees together and let them fall open.

He jerks as if I've struck him. "What the hell are you doing?"

My face is burning now, but I can't let that deter me, not when my safety is on the line. "You said I have to hold up my end of this deal, so I'm ready to do that. But you'll have to do most of the work because I'm not entirely sure what to do. Well, I understand the logistics, of course, but I've never…"

I trail off because the look on his face is nothing short of murderous.

## 13

## ADRIAN

I pull my hand from hers and put the distance of the room between us. The bathroom door is closed. I don't go that far since I still need to be able to see her. Even while she's in no shape to enjoy herself, I'm three seconds from taking everything she offers. The fire that's burned in my blood for her since the moment we met rages through me, demanding I make her mine, and I fear I won't be able to hold out long. Especially with her baring herself to me, offering everything I want.

"Are you okay?" she asks, hesitant and scared all over again because of me.

I face her and shake my head, relieved to see she'd closed her thighs, leaving only her knees and lower legs bare. My eyes trace down to the bandages around her ankles, and it works as effectively as a bucket of ice water on my system. I go back to the bed, but this time, I don't touch her. "I'm fine. There are some things we need to discuss, and things we will do to settle our debt, but not yet."

She doesn't even bother not to look relieved. The offer was nothing more than to finish things between us. If she were anyone else, I could appreciate her sheer practicality. I'd never shied away from doing what was necessary, if even distasteful, to take care of business. But she's not anyone else with that hair, and those eyes, and her sweet little body I've seen more than I can handle since I saved her life.

I focus on her face, ignoring the relief to watch for any other signs. "You believe me when I say we won't go to bed together until you're feeling better."

She shrugs, and I shift up the bed until I can look into her eyes, only inches from her face. "I don't like lies. It's what drew me to you in the first place. As long as you're honest with me, I'll be honest with you. Tell me you understand."

She clears her injured throat gently. "I understand," she whispers.

I tilt her chin up so I can stare into her big doe eyes, hunting for the conviction I saw at the party that night. At the conviction I saw when she came to me for aid. "I have no reason to lie to you. Trust me, I intend to take you to bed, just not right now."

This time, she nods, and I take her word she believes me. What else can I do? I release her chin and check her bandages. Everything is still in place, and I can breathe a little easier. "The IV was placed in there because you needed nutrients. I can take it out now if you'd like?"

She gives me another nod, this one more urgent. I get up and gather the alcohol swabs and a Band-Aid. I've had so many IVs and given a few myself, so removing hers is nothing. She doesn't even flinch as I clean the tiny puncture wound and place the waterproof bandage over it.

"How are you feeling?" I ask, needing something to focus on besides the creamy pink of her inner thighs.

"Fine. But I feel kind of gross. I want to take a shower."

"I've been giving you sponge baths since I brought you here, but taking a bath would be good. You don't have any open wounds now, and if you soak in some Epsom salt, it will help bring down some of your bruising."

I look up to find her smiling at me. No guile, no subterfuge, nothing but pure light. And damn, how I'm going to take it for myself. "How do you know that? About soaking in the salt, I mean."

"You met me at the casino when we had a fight. You're too young to know that I used to be a fighter. My father thought it would help beef me up."

She raises an eyebrow at that, pointedly staring at my shoulders and arms.

"This was when I was nothing more than a kid. I hadn't hit my growth spurt, nor had I taken up lifting yet."

I secure the IV so it doesn't leak, and then come around the bed to scoop her up into my arms. She wraps her hands around my neck. The bandages scratch against my skin, but I don't care, not with so much of her body against mine.

She weighs nothing as I carry her to the bathroom, and I worry she won't be able to handle me. I'm not giving her up, but I'll have to be gentle, careful with her so I don't hurt her. Even more so than I usually try to be with women.

I set her gently on the marble surround of the tub and turn on the water. Then I dig out the Epsom salt, pour in a generous amount, and turn to her. Her cheeks are flaming pink, and it hits me that she's embarrassed.

I brush her fumbling fingers aside, then quickly unhook the buttons down the shirt and peel it off her shoulders. With equal practicality, despite the hard-on digging against my fly, I gently unwind the gauze from her wrists and ankles to find the skin is still bright pink. Seeing the bruises from the ropes cools the heat in my blood enough for me to focus on her.

She stares down at her wrists and gently touches her left one. I can tell she wants to know what happened, but she's not brave enough to ask yet. Until she is, she won't be able to handle it, nor what I'm going to do to Sal when I get my hands on him.

I gently lift her again, and she gives a little squeal of surprise. Then I slowly lower her into the water, even as it climbs higher, wetting my sleeves and shirt.

Once she's settled in the tub, I release her, and she lets out a long sigh. "That feels good."

The needy hint in her voice doesn't help my erection. Fucking focus.

I grab some of my shampoo from the shower stall on the other end of the bathroom and set it on the marble. "I'm going to wash your hair now."

She eases forward in the tub and bites her lip as she looks at the bottle.

"What? You don't like this brand?"

"It's not that. It's just that my hair maintenance is complicated. The curls and all require extra care."

I put the bottle down and kneel beside the tub. "Then tell me what to do. I'll be taking care of you from now on, so I need to know things like this."

She studies me, as if gauging my sincerity, then decides in my favor I guess since she continues. "Well, wash it, then I have to use a lot of conditioner before you brush it out. It's not a big deal if it dries on its own or anything. It's not like I can go anywhere with all these bruises."

I gently nudge her back into the water, and she wets her hair. It doesn't take long to wash it, then I follow her instructions to condition it and brush it out, careful not to pull at her scalp. Once satisfied, she nods and leans back on the tub. "I just need to let it sit for a second before we rinse."

The way she says we sends another surge of need through me. I'm already barely hanging on to my control after digging my hands into her hair as she moaned her pleasure with every press of my fingers.

She washes her body even though I offer, and then I help her rinse. Once her skin is a soft glowing pink, dotted with bruises, I strip out of my soaking wet clothes and wrap her in a towel.

Her eyes are wide as I carry her back to the bed. My towel is huge around her shoulders, covering her from collarbone to ankle.

"Why is that look on your face? I'm not going to hurt you now that you're bathed."

She shakes her head frantically and lets out a small laugh. "It's not that. You're just pretty naked."

I glance down at my navy boxer briefs. "Pretty sure you're more naked than I am."

With her averting her gaze, I grumble, quickly change the sheets, and then gently dry her skin. She protests, but I block it all with a shake of my head. It pleases me when she goes silent, watching me but not scared.

Once she's dry, I pull out a soft cotton thing that Andrea picked out. It looks like it will cover her to her mid-thighs. The white is lovely on her as I cover all the curves I want so much more than a look at. I kneel on the floor to help her into soft white cotton panties that match her nightgown.

My fingers are shaking as I settle the fabric in place against her delicate hip bones.

"Are you okay? Was I too heavy?"

I give her a look and a snort. "You weigh nothing. Lie back on the pillows and get comfortable."

She does as ordered, already looking so much better than when I found her almost two weeks ago.

"What are you going to do?"

I nod at the chair. "Sleep, just like you will."

She shifts in the bed and pats the empty space beside her. "Stay, please. I already feel guilty for taking your bed. I'll feel even worse if you hurt your back sleeping in that chair."

I do it only because I'm dying to touch her again. I need it like I need to breathe. If only to reassure myself she will be okay. I ease onto the bed, taking up way more space than she expected. Her eyes rove over my body, and I like the look in her eyes as she trails her gaze down my abs to the waist of my underwear.

I'm so hard that my blood is pounding in my ears. Fuck. I thought I was stronger than this. But I'm not where she is concerned. I take her small hand in my hand and wrap her fingers around my thumb.

She blinks, confused, but does.

"Squeeze," I grit out.

Again, she follows directions with no hesitation. My breathing is coming out loud enough to drown out all the other noises. "How does that feel? And don't lie to me."

"Fine?"

"Any pain?"

She shakes her head. "You might have noticed," she whispers. "I have a somewhat high pain tolerance."

I don't ask her to explain that statement. I only add one more tally to Sal's growing debt to her. A debt I'll extract in blood.

"Good," I say and ease my underwear off my legs and toss them to the floor. She's staring now, wide-eyed, right at my cock, and I keep the moan inside as I wrap her hand around me. She hesitates at first, but then I see the curiosity chase across her expressive face. I cover her hand with mine and use my other to lift her chin to meet my eyes. "I'm not going to hurt you, but I need to take the edge off so I stay in control."

She only nods and swallows loudly. I watch her face as I ease her hand up toward the crown of my dick and then back down. She's curious, and by the way she's squeezing her thighs together, she's feeling other things too. The knowledge I could roll her over and sink into her wet heat sends me to the edge far too quickly.

"Harder," I grit out. "Squeeze me as hard as you can."

She starts to pull away from under my hold. "I don't want to hurt you."

I meet her eyes again. "You won't hurt me. This will make me feel good. I need it so I don't take you right here, right now. Please." It's the closest I've ever come, or will come, to asking her for what belongs to me.

She nods once and eases her hand back down. I clamp mine tighter around hers, adding the other one. "Am I hurting you?" I ask, between pants.

"No." She continues the strokes, increasing the pace and squeezing harder as she gets to know the feel of me. It's this knowledge that makes me shoot my load hard and fast. It's not nearly as satisfying as I need it to be. I release her hand, but she continues stroking me, spreading my cum down my shaft and back up. One more and then she stops, looking at me for instructions.

I get the damp towel I used to dry her off and clean her hand gently, ensuring her wrist wound is clean and safe.

Then I clean myself and settle in the bed. She turns on her side and allows me to spoon my body against hers.

I'm almost asleep, assuming she'd drifted off way before me, when she speaks again. "I think I liked that. I just don't know why." Her voice turns dreamy. "I have to tell Rose."

And it breaks my fucking heart that she sounds both scared and sad at that fact.

## 14

## VALENTINA

*I*f I don't get out of this bed, I'm going to go insane. When it's time to eat, Adrian wants to feed me. When it's time to clean myself, Adrian is there to carry me. When it's time to see the doctor, Adrian hovers, waiting for the verdict. It's not that I don't appreciate the tender care he's given me so far; it's just that I'm not used to not doing anything.

I also don't trust it all. This can't be the deal we made, him waiting on me hand and foot, and no doubt paying an obscene amount of money to the doctor who visits almost every day. He keeps telling me not to worry about anything, but I worry, and I worry some more about when the other shoe is going to drop, and when the other side of him that everyone is so afraid of will come out. He's been nothing but kind to me, and that's the problem. I've been trapped my whole life, a lamb in the lion's den, and I won't be that girl ever again.

The doctor checks my vitals one more time and then tucks his stethoscope around his neck. He doesn't speak to me but turns to Adrian with his report. "She's perfectly fine. Healing well, no infection. She can get out of bed."

Relief hits me hard, and I immediately want to jerk back the covers and stand on my own two feet.

Adrian glares over the doctor's shoulder, a look that's more order than him using actual words. So I stay put. When he speaks, he talks to the doctor. "It's been two weeks since she woke up. Are you sure it's safe for her to be up and around?"

There's no missing the edge in his tone. A sharp bite that makes me sink into the covers. Not that I fear he'll turn it on me, but again, I'm waiting for things to change around here. For me to turn into some kind of slave for his fetishes. I don't look at him while I think this because heaven knows I have no clue what a real fetish might be. Foot stuff? I press my knuckles to my mouth so I don't laugh out loud and interrupt their conversation.

They lower their voices, and Adrian still has that nip to his tone, which the doctor seems oblivious to. Once they finish talking, the doctor leaves the room without a single word to me. I guess I know where I stand on the hierarchy here.

Then I notice he's looking at me. I gulp and shift my gaze to him as he approaches the bed and slides in beside me. "The doctor says you are well enough to get out of bed."

"I feel okay if that helps ease your mind. I know you're worried."

He raises one dark eyebrow at my assumption, and I stammer out an explanation. "I mean, you seem worried. Not that I don't appreciate you taking care of me, I just don't want you to keep worrying."

His fingers grip my chin and raise my gaze to his in a split second. My mouth goes dry as his eyes lock with mine. "It is my job to worry about you now. It's your job to trust me to take care of you and keep you safe."

Safe. It seems like a foreign concept. He's the only one who has ever made me feel even close to it. His thumb digs into the bottom of my chin, demanding my attention.

I nod once, as much as I can in his hold. "I understand."

His eyes narrow. "I understand isn't the same as I believe you. Say it for me. Tell me you believe that I can keep you safe."

I want to believe it, and if I want to believe something, I'm very good at tricking myself into thinking it's true. "I know you can keep me safe."

He's still gripping my chin a little too tight, and there's still a hungry glint in his eyes, but he doesn't make the demand again. "Since the doctor has given you the all clear, then we have business to settle."

Shit. My heart starts a running leap against my ribs. "Business?"

Is he going to make me strip for him again? For his men? Will he use me like Sal wanted to use me? The image of my hand around him rushes back to me. We've done that multiple times now but never more. He never pushes me for anything else. Maybe because he worried I'd get hurt.

I shake off the sudden spike of fear, forcing myself to remember, yet again, that he's been wonderful to me since I arrived. He saved me.

"We need to discuss our deal and what it means for our future."

The way he says our future makes me study his face. He's staring down at me just as intently.

"Okay. Tell me what you expect of me then, please. I want you to be happy with our deal." I want him to be happy because I want Sal's blood running down a storm drain until there's nothing left of the asshole. My vehemence surprises me, but I shake it off and focus on Adrian again.

"You will belong to me and only to me. No one will touch you. No one will so much as breathe too close to you. Do I make myself clear?"

I nod, about to say so, but he continues. "I'll know where you are every second of every single day. It's the only way I can keep you safe."

I'm tempted to point out that if he kills Sal, then there's no one else he needs to protect me from. It's not like my father can stand up to him physically. He could send one of his soldiers, but even they are getting older. In the past year, it seemed to me he only held on to the family seat because of Sal's men and the ruthlessness they brought to the table.

"Is that all?" I ask. Having him protect me doesn't sound so bad. "What about...?"

"Sex?" he offers, his tone dry.

I nod, unable to expound on my train of thought.

"We'll be having plenty of it soon. Don't you worry."

My heart takes another go at my ribs, pounding hard and fast. "Um...I-I've never done...that."

Something shifts in his face. It's subtle, but there's a harder glint in his eyes now as he looks at me. No. Covets me. "I'm aware, Angel, but don't worry. I'll take good care of you."

His words are innocuous, but the deep huskiness in his voice makes them sound positively filthy. I shift in the bed, hoping he can't tell that I like it when he talks like that. Who the hell am I turning into?

I drag my eyes away from his and stare at the covers. "Is there anything else you want from me? If not, then I still agree to this deal. I...trust you."

Without a word, he shifts off the bed, goes back to the door, and waves the doctor back into the room. I sit up, arranging the covers around my hips. Why is he back?

The doctor gives him one nod and crosses the room to stand by the bed to look at me. "Are you sure about this?"

I eye him warily. "Yes. I'm sure, but..."

He opens his bag and removes something that looks like an ear-piercing gun. I stare at it a little too long and then over the doctor's shoulder at Adrian, who's watching us closely.

The doctor grabs my arm gently and maneuvers it to my wrist and palm face upward. It might be my long-dormant self-preservation instincts kicking up, but I jerk my hand away from him hard.

"Valentina," Adrian snaps.

He hasn't used that tone of voice with me, and for a flash of a second, it felt like being at home. Fear threatens to overwhelm me, and I'm suddenly scrambling over the other side of the bed to get away.

Of course, he's there in an instant, carefully, but bodily putting me back into the bed and holding me down.

I don't know what the hell is happening, but I agreed to this.

I agreed to this.

I agreed to this.

I agree—

"Ow, oh my God." I stare down at the tiny well of blood on my forearm as the doctor packs the device in his bag again. Then he swipes the wound with an alcohol swab that sends another bolt of pain into my elbow. He applies a bandage and I jerk my arm up into my chest the best I can with Adrian on me and glare at him. The man doesn't seem to care as he gathers himself and leaves again.

I turn my accusing gaze to Adrian, but he's staring at me with the same hungry feral gaze he had when I met him at the casino. It terrifies me and sets things on fire at the same time. I blink and wait for him to sit on the bed again. "What the hell was that?"

"A microchip. I told you I'll know where you are every second of every day. This will ensure I can keep you safe. No one else will have access to the data except me. Not even my men."

I'm about two seconds from bolting again, but...I agreed to this. He eases his weight off me and sits down on the bed near my splayed knees.

To my relief, he doesn't force me to lie down again. I guess if I'm well enough to have something implanted in me, then I'm well enough to sit up on my own. Another thought hits me hard, and it scares me.

"When you're done with me, are you going to let me go?" I'm not brave enough to look at him when I ask.

He drags my eyes to his again, and there's something deadly there.

"Understand this now. I will never let you go. You belong to me and only to me."

I blink at the vehemence in his voice. The sheer conviction spoken in a silken caress reminds me once again that I made this happen. This deal is mine. So I nod because I don't have any words to explain what's happening in my brain and in my body right now.

When I can speak, I turn on the bed and offer my hands to him. "Then I'm ready. Are we going to have sex here, or did you want to go somewhere else that doesn't smell like a hospital room?"

A tiny smile plays at the corner of his mouth, and it mesmerizes me.

"We aren't having sex right now, Angel. Don't worry. Some things need to be taken care of before I sink inside your little pussy for the first time."

Heat flashes through me again at his words, pooling at my core, reminding me yet again how he felt clutched tight in my hands.

He tipped my chin up and leaned down to nuzzle the side of my neck. I can't even help leaning into him. The scent of him, his warm skin, everything about him draws me in and comforts me.

"As the only man who will ever be inside you, I plan to take my time. Sometimes, little Angel, I'll be gentle with you, and others, I'll take my pleasure from you as surely as I'll force yours upon you."

His voice rumbles against my skin now, turning the hot flash of need into something deeper, warmer. Each word he speaks stokes it higher until I can feel it in my breasts, my cheeks, my ears even.

I squeeze my thighs together, knowing it won't quench the fire he's started. Even after everything I've gone through, every beating, every humiliation, every trauma, he makes me feel...something. I'm not sure what it is. Safe doesn't seem a big enough word, and loved is a joke, considering we've only known each other a month or so.

It takes me a moment to realize he's staring down at me expectantly. "Sorry, I got distracted."

When he licks his lips, I'm lost all over again.

"Listen to me. Are you listening?"

I nod and meet his eyes so I can actually do what he says.

"Right now, we are going to take a shower while the staff comes in and cleans up. Then we'll make arrangements for our wedding. Once you have my name and my official protection...then I'm going to sink deep into that hot cunt of yours. After that happens, there's no going back for either of us."

My mouth hangs open as he scoops me into his arms and carries me into the bathroom.

*Married. To him?*

## 15

# ADRIAN

Despite the doctor's clean bill of health, and her insistence that she's fine, I try to keep her in bed as much as possible for another week. By the end of it, she's going stir-crazy, and it grates on my nerves. There is one thing we need to go over before we can complete the ceremony. The ceremony my team has been setting up while I kept her confined so she doesn't make a run for it. She agreed to our deal, but I'm not sure she has a full understanding of her place in my life now.

I need to ensure she understands, and I need to know exactly what Sal and her father did to her. Both of them will die when I get my hands on them, but I need to know exactly how much pain to inflict before their last breaths leave their bodies. I can already feel Sal's neck under my hands, and I can't wait to squeeze his throat until his eyeballs bulge out of his greasy little head.

A hand brushes my shoulder, and I snap my gaze up. Valentina is there with a look of concern etched over her features. "Are you all right? You looked upset for a moment."

I shake off the reverie and focus on her. Instead of eating in the bedroom, I brought her to the dining room for breakfast today. She gave my stainless steel, granite, and glass décor a quick once-over before sitting down. But I can't read her well enough to tell if she approves.

We've finished eating, and I asked her to remain so we can talk. The staff has cleared out, and my team is still preparing for the ceremony.

She watches me carefully, and I shift to grab the edge of her chair. Her little squeak of surprise echoes through the room as I drag the chair close to me, so close she must part her thighs to keep from touching my legs with hers.

Only once she's met my eyes do I speak. "Now, we need to discuss your father and your—Sal. I need you to tell me what they did to you. Everything from the first time your father raised his hand to you to the moment I saved you from the house."

Her forehead bunches hard as she drags her eyes away to stare at the table. "I...Well, it started after my mother died. He sort of changed. With her death, the loving father I'd grown to know just disappeared. Suddenly, everything I did was wrong. His brutality worsened as I got older."

She speaks in a matter-of-fact tone as if she's already resigned herself to that abuse, and it didn't matter. I suppose after ten years or so, it wouldn't anymore. Not if you had to live with it every day.

"And Sal?" I prompt. "When did that start?"

This subject isn't as easy for her. She swallows heavily and wrings her hands in her lap. "On my eighteenth birthday, my father announced I was engaged and introduced me to Sal. He made it very clear that if I didn't marry him, Rose and I would be thrown out without a penny to my name, and he'd do his best to ruin any effort I made to stand on my own."

I clench my fists but try not to show her the rage pouring through me in a slow trickle.

She continues, and I catalog every single word. "It started innocuously. He'd touch me inappropriately. Well, he didn't think it was wrong since we were engaged. That's when my father made it a rule that he couldn't sleep with me until we married." She lets out a rueful chuckle. "Probably the only nice thing my father ever did for me. Anyway, once he couldn't get a sexual release from me, he started beating me and showing me videos of the most hideous things. He'd take videos of him hurting me, and—" She cuts off with a gasp, and I scan her features for a clue as to what's wrong.

"Sal, he…" Her voice quakes, and she blinks several times. Then she wraps her arms around herself and starts a slow rocking back and forth. "He…and…Rose."

A sob rips from her lips as tears pour down her pale cheeks. "Rose," she says one more time.

I gather her into my arms and hold her sideways across my lap. Her memory must be coming back now, and all I can do is comfort her until I show her proof of Sal's death.

A few seconds pass as she cries softly, and then she wriggles in my grip and shoves at my chest. "You, you didn't tell me Rose was dead. You let me think she was still out there, alive and safe."

I narrow my eyes and grip her forearms to keep from her beating at my chest with her small hands. "First of all, don't speak to me that way." I keep my tone calm and even, and it seems to settle her back into my lap. "Second, I never once said a thing about Rose or where she was. I simply didn't give you any details about your rescue as I wasn't sure where things were in your memory."

Another sob shudders out of her, and I release her forearms to gather her up again. For a second, she pushes against me to get free, but I won't let her go, not while she faces the truth of what happened to her.

"Is there anything else? Can you tell me what Sal did to you that night? The last time you saw him?"

Her voice is garbled from tears and snot when she answers. "He beat me. I snuck back inside, and he'd already ra—hurt Rose, and then he came for me."

The doctor did an examination, so I know that even though Sal raped her cousin, he didn't touch her that way. He'd harmed her just fine without the additional torture, but for some reason, he didn't take that final step in his game.

I still haven't figured out if he thought he could go back to the house and resume his relationship with her and marry her as planned.

Before I try to puzzle it out some more, my phone digs in my pocket. She stiffens in my grip, and I stand with her still tucked tight in my arms. "I'm sorry that we didn't get to finish talking," I tell her, "but we have an appointment to keep. I'll take you upstairs so you can get ready. Andrea will help you."

Her face is tear-streaked and pale, but it doesn't matter. She's still achingly beautiful to me. I nuzzle my face against her neck and breathe in her scent. "Wear your hair down for me." I don't bother saying please. It's nothing less than an order, and if she doesn't release it before I watch her walk down the aisle, I'll do it myself.

I leave her with Andrea and go to my office to get ready. It doesn't take me long to put on the tuxedo and dig out the ring box from my bottom desk drawer. As I walk out to the command center, I wonder if I should feel nervous. I don't. From the second I saw her, I knew she belonged to me. A wedding will give her a certain level of protection from society. It will also ensure Sal or her father don't try to claim her once they realize I have her.

The ceremony is small; Kai and my five plus the minister are all that's necessary. I watch her walk down the aisle, a white silk dress hugging every inch of her body. Her hair is unbound but pushed away from her face by some kind of sparkly hair accessory.

She's wearing makeup now, but it doesn't hide the red rim of her eyes nor the wet sheen on her cheeks. But she walks down the aisle of her own volition and makes her vows without any prompting. She knows this is her best shot at staying safe. I only hope I can convince her that in time, things will be different between us.

We eat dinner alone in the dining room, and she barely pushes food around her plate. This I can't have. I pull a chair beside her and take her fork. She doesn't even protest, as if all the fight has gone out of her.

"Look at me," I snap.

Her red eyes lock on mine.

"You've endured everything they put you through. Don't let them break you now that you're free."

She stares down at her plate again. "Am I, though? I've traded one kind of captivity for another."

I grab her chin hard and force her to look at me. "I won't tolerate talk like that. We made a deal, and I expect you to honor it. As I will honor my side. You agreed to this. I didn't force you for a single moment."

She blinks a few times, and her shoulders slump. "You're right. I know. But I can't stop seeing Rose's eyes in my head now that I remember. They won't go away, and I don't know if it's better to have just forgotten her death." She sighs and tucks her fist against her chest like she's trying to hold her heart inside. "It certainly hurt less."

The image of my father's vacant eyes hits me, but I shove it away, the same as I always do. "If you aren't going to eat, then we should go to bed."

She nods, and I pick her up before she can inch out of her chair. When we reach the bedroom, I set her on the side of the bed and find the zipper of her dress to help her out of it.

"It was a pretty dress," she whispers. "Thank you for thinking of it. The flowers and the minister were also nice. I know you didn't have a lot of time to prepare."

I don't respond to her thank you because I'm too busy staring down at all the pinky pale skin revealed after removing the dress. She's only wearing a scrap of lace for panties and nothing else. Her breasts are full enough that I can fill my palms, and I do it since I can't stop thinking about touching more of her.

I thumb her nipple with one hand while I rip my bow tie off with the other. Then I shrug out of my jacket, kick off my shoes, and finish undressing in seconds. Her eyes are wide and scared as I crawl onto the bed naked. She's so small compared to me, and I don't want to hurt her.

She lies back on the pillows, and tears start sliding down her cheeks again. I lean over her, propped on my elbow, and slide my hand over her smooth belly. Soon, my child will grow there, and I can't wait to see if my son has curls like hers.

Her hard sniffle makes me scan her face again. Seeing her cry does something to me. I hate it more than anything. Each sob wrenches a tiny bit of my sanity loose until I can't take not touching her, comforting her.

I drag her into my arms and curl around her back. "Calm down, Angel. I'm not going to force you. We'll keep things slow, but understand, we will keep moving forward. You belong to me now, and I want everything from you."

She sniffles again, and I lean in and rub my nose up the curve of her neck. Then I press my face into her nape, her soft curls brushing my cheeks. "I want your joy," I murmur, burrowing deeper against her. "I want your tears. I want your pain. I want your pleasure. It all belongs to me. And you'll give it to me before I take you."

Despite my declaration, one niggling thread of doubt winds through my head. Every minute Sal is alive is another minute I haven't held up my end of the deal. It's another minute she might think of leaving me, and I'll never allow her to go.

## 16

## VALENTINA

*I* can't stop crying, and every time I so much as sniffle, Adrian stiffens and his fingers tighten on me. Remembering my cousin and best friend is dead a few minutes before I have to walk down the aisle is not how I imagined my wedding day. Hell, none of this is how I imagined my wedding day. But to be fair, I'd avoided thinking about it because my fiancé was never my choice. Despite my tears and the sorrow rolling through me, Adrian is my choice.

It might not be a marriage in the traditional sense, but I am trying to believe he'll keep me safe. Even from himself. I swipe at the tears on my cheeks and blink up at his face. This probably isn't the wedding night he envisioned either. His fingers dig into my hips—not painfully, but it feels like he's waiting. If it's a holding pattern for me to be ready for sex, it's definitely not happening.

All over again, Rose's face flashes in my head, and another round of tears starts pouring out of my eyes. Adrian tugs me tight into his chest so I'm lying with our legs intertwined and my lips almost against his sternum. So much of his bare skin drags me from my grief. I latch onto it, pressing my fingers into his very solid pecs. There's a slight smattering of dark hair across them, but it's soft against my cheek.

I focus on his skin and breathing. Hoping it's enough to keep my thoughts on hold so I can stop crying.

"I understand you're upset," he says, his voice deep and rumbling in the confined space between us. "But you're stronger than this. You need to be stronger than this."

It's not a censure; his voice isn't hard or scolding. He says it matter-of-factly, and somehow, it's his frank tone that makes me scrub the tears away again and lift my chin to look at his face.

He's staring down at me, and there's no pity in his gaze. No sympathy yet no give either. I swallow hard and whisper, "I don't want to have sex right now. I just can't."

"It's our wedding night."

I move to push away from his hold, but he tightens his grip. A spike of fear shoots through me. Is this when he shows his true colors and turns into someone like my father, someone like Sal?

No sooner does the thought drift into my head does he shove me away hard and climb off the bed. It takes me a second to catch up, then I sit up to study him. If I don't watch him, I can't protect myself if he comes at me.

But he doesn't. He only paces back and forth at the end of the bed, clenching his fists. I've made him angry because I won't sleep with him. I realize this is a part of our deal, but the thought of sex right now, after the memory of Sal's hands on my naked body burned its way into my brain only a couple of hours ago, sickens me. It physically makes me nauseated.

I swipe more tears away, impatiently, and watch him pace. Should I apologize? Throw myself down on the floor and beg him not to take what he's already bargained to have? I thought I'd accepted what is happening between us, but now, on the other side of my memories resurfacing, it all feels so much heavier, so much more real.

And I want Sal so much more dead. It hits me all over that his death is why I made this deal. Why I married a stranger today, and why I'm currently sitting in his bed in only a scrap of lace. I can't risk him backing out on that because I can't kill him. As evident by the fact that he almost killed me, and I barely put up a fight.

"I'm sorry," I say barely above a whisper.

I have no idea if he hears me or if he's just ignoring me, but he doesn't stop his pacing. Tears squeeze out of my eyes again, and then he swipes a lamp off a side table, and it hits the floor in a shattering crash.

I scurry to the top of the bed, huddling in the pillows. He whirls toward the bed, bracing his fists on the end of it to look up the length at me. "I haven't touched you."

His tone makes me want to put the pillows between us, but I don't, knowing it might anger him more. I'd seen it so many times with my father. The more I defended myself, the angrier he got.

"I know," I venture. "I know. I'm sorry."

He throws his hands up this time. "Stop fucking apologizing. I didn't ask you to apologize. What I need from you is proof you understand I'm not going to hurt you. Have I done so in the weeks you've been with me?"

I shake my head, a spike of guilt cutting through me. "No, you haven't. I'm so—I mean, you've been nothing but kind. This isn't about you."

His eyes are hard. "Explain."

I swallow and wet my lips. "I have never been around a man who can control his anger, or at the very least not direct it at me. Every time you get upset, I expect you to take your fury out on me. It's not you. With the memories coming back, and the wedding, and you being so..." I wave at his nudity. Every freaking glorious inch of him. "I'm overwhelmed."

It's a shit explanation, but it's all I have to give.

He stalks away, and more glass hits the floor in a crash. This time, I stay still, watching him warily. But true to his word, he doesn't approach me or make demands of me.

The spike of guilt turns sharper, digging in like a splinter. I dry my face on the blanket, leaving a makeup smudge, but I don't care. Then I carefully climb off the bed, moving slowly to approach him.

When I reach him, he stills with his back to me. I reach out and touch the back of his shoulder gently. He doesn't move and doesn't even seem to be breathing. For a second, I want to take my hand back, return to the bed, and hide under the covers until he decides what to do with me. But I don't.

The memories came back to me, but along with it are the memories of him. The one where he cut loose the bindings Sal had tied me down with. And how he gently lifted me into his arms and carried me out of there. Since then, he's been with me constantly, caring for me, helping me recover. I have to remember those facts—not just the trauma but also the blessings.

I lay my hand flat against his warm skin and run my fingers across his wide shoulders. He seems impossibly large. He has since the moment I met him, but naked and angry, he seems bigger.

When he doesn't shove me away, I hesitantly put my other hand on his skin, marveling at the width of his shoulder blades under my palms. Then I curve them out over the tops of his shoulders to his biceps. As I do this, I step into his back and press my lips to the rigid length of his spine, and whisper, "I'm sorry."

He sweeps me into his arms before I can even react to his turning to face me. Once again, he carries me to the bed as if I weigh nothing and sets me down on the rumpled covers. I wait to see what he'll do, not wanting to anger him further.

Some of the tension seems to have left his shoulders, though, and he's no longer clenching and unclenching his fists like he can't wait to pummel something. He gathers me back into his arms and moves me onto his lap. My head barely reaches his chin, and I must tilt it to look up at him. It's easier to try to gauge his mood when I can see his face. Not that he gives much away.

"I won't hurt you," he tells me for the hundredth time.

In answer, I press my forehead into his chest and breathe him in, letting the smoky scent of him take me back to the night we met. The night I gained the tiniest glimmer of hope. The night that changed everything.

He gently eases me back onto the bed and settles between my thighs. I tense under him, but he makes no move to take off my panties, nor does he rub against me even though I can feel the hard length of him everywhere.

I have the tiniest moment to wonder what he's going to do when he leans down and kisses me gently. It's more than the kiss he gave me at the altar only a couple of hours ago. Somehow, even though it's just his lips against mine, it contains the promise of so much more.

"Touch me," he orders. "If you don't want me to rip off this underwear and bury my cock inside you, touch me now."

I run my hands over his shoulders and down to his biceps, then easing my hands underneath to curl around his waist to the solid muscles of his back. "Is that okay?"

"More."

A wash of heat hits my neck as I ease my hands down to the top of his ass. There's a sharp curve where his back gives way to the round softness of his butt, and I like it. I ease my fingers over him and then back up. "Where else do you want me to touch you?"

I realize it's a stupid question once I've asked it. Where do I think he wants me to touch him? The evidence of his need is very thick and very much poking into my belly. "If you want me to touch you there, you'll have to move off me."

He carefully eases away and settles into the pillow, one knee propped up, his hardness leaning against his rock-solid abs. I take my time looking at him before crawling closer and settling next to his hip.

He curls his hand around my thigh, watching me. "Touch me." This time his voice is gentle, the edge of a plea, but not quite so far as all that. I reach out and grip him hard, remembering he likes me to squeeze him. He drops his head back on the pillow and lets his eyes drift shut. Once I tear my gaze away from his face, I focus on my task.

Tonight, he's giving me the gift of time, of space, and I should thank him for it. I ease closer and stare down at him, trying to figure out how to do what I have in mind. But I can't figure it out, so I shrug, hunch over, and lap at the dark purple crown above my grip.

He hisses out a breath and jerks his head up to stare at me. When he doesn't make a move to stop me, I lick him again, turning my face so I can see his reactions.

"Take me between your lips, Angel. You're not going to hurt me."

I do as directed and slide my mouth around his thick cock. He tastes salty, but not in a bad way, and I spend a minute testing how far I can ease him into the back of my throat. It's not far until the weight of his hand tangles in my curls, and he urges me a little farther.

He groans, and tears spring to my eyes, but I let him take control. He fists my hair and drags my head up and down, up and down. I grab his thighs for something to hold while he uses me for his pleasure. It's filthy, a little bit painful, and so damn hot I can feel my answering wetness between my thighs.

He groans again, and the sound shoots through me in a new way. I focus on keeping my teeth out of the way while he increases his tempo. When his next thrust makes me gag, he gives one more hard push into my mouth, and then he comes. It surprises me, and I only swallow a little before the rest drizzles out of my lips and down my chin.

With the weight of his hand gone, I lift up and wipe my face with the back of my hand. His eyes are closed, and his chest is heaving like he just ran a marathon.

"Are you okay?" I ask.

He pops one eye open, snags me around the waist, and draws me into the curve of his arm. "I'm wonderful, Angel. Lie here and get some rest for now."

I curl up against him, and for the first time in hours, my mind is blissfully calm and clear. I'm asleep before the lights even go out.

# 17

# ADRIAN

*I* know I shouldn't be around my team today. Not touching her, not taking her has grated my nerves raw. When she cries, though, I can't resist comforting her and watching the light come back into her eyes. Nor can I stand the thought of being the one who finally extinguishes that light.

I'm thankful none of my men offer any smart-ass remarks as I take my seat at the table. Kai, dressed to kill as usual, throws himself into the chair beside me. "Nothing yet."

They all know why I'm here when I should be enjoying myself between my new wife's thighs right now. "Not even any leads?"

Kai pulls out his phone and passes it to me. "I have eyes on everything and everywhere he might want to go."

I squeeze the phone and then hand it back before I crush it. "The bastard can't hide forever. I want him flushed out and locked down so I can deal with him." Kai knows the terms of my marriage, but none of the others do…yet. I'm not in the mood to enlighten them.

"What about her father? Any movement on that front? He hasn't made any effort to contact his daughter or his niece?"

Kai leans forward to try to catch my eye. No doubt trying to read my mood. It should be fucking obvious. "Not that we can tell. According to the staff we were able to talk to, they have a strained relationship. He barely speaks to her some days, and others, well...let's just say he needs to be gutted."

I close my eyes and breathe for a moment, needing to rein in my temper. My friends aren't at fault here. "What about the rest of society? Any changes since the season started?"

Andrea, with her big sweet eyes that disarm everyone, spoke up first. "Alexei and I have been monitoring any shifts. So far, no one's made any big moves, but I swear, boss, every time we show our faces at an event, we get mobbed by people asking about you. I swear one of the mothers practically shoved her daughter's tits in Alexei's face to try to entice him into putting in a good word."

Alexei, the darker, harder version of his sister, shrugged. "They were pretty nice. Of course, I was vague and made a quick exit. I should have told them to put the boobs in Andrea's face. She might have appreciated the peep show as much as me."

Andrea shrugs and gives us all a wink. "We'll keep an eye on it. Right now, we are also trying to get more information on what business is keeping Valentina's father so busy out of town."

I nod, some of my anger fizzling with it. "What is staying with me is why didn't Sal go with him? He usually goes on those sorts of trips."

Ivan, my quiet muscle, fields this question. "Also something we are trying to figure out. It might just be he wanted time to—" He breaks off. He was there the day we brought Valentina home.

I study my hands, thinking. "He's not smart enough to plan. I wonder if there was something else, and he just saw the opportunity. I feel like we're missing something, and I hate this feeling."

Everyone shifts uneasily. I make it my business to know everything. If I don't, then I can't make an informed decision, and it's the only kind of decision I make.

"Back to Sal. Tell me about his situation. Was he staying in the house with the family?"

Kai catches my attention. "Sometimes, not full time, mostly when the father needed him for business, or if there was an event that they needed to attend together."

The memory of Sal touching Valentina hits me hard, and I curl my fists against my thigh. "What about money? His family needs it. That was why he wanted to marry her, right? If we offer the family enough money, do you think they would turn on him? Offer up his hiding place in exchange?"

I meet Kai's eyes, waiting for the answer. "I think they might pretend they will. They'd be happy to take your money, and then they'll give us a false location or a false trail just to fuck with us."

"Make the offer and see what happens. I want to know if they will bite or ignore it."

Kai nods, even if he doesn't look happy about the choice. Hell, I'm not happy about it either, but it's made, and I don't go back on my decisions.

I need to calm down and get back to Valentina. The sooner she feels at ease with me, the sooner I can start winning her heart. And she has no idea yet, but sex will be one of the weapons I use.

I shove to stand and survey my team. "I don't care what it costs. Find him, and bring him here."

A rush of air behind me alerts me to the door opening. At first, I expect the cook, who brings coffee for the carafe we keep here. But it's not her, it's Valentina. She's wrapped in one of my dress shirts, which covers her from neck to knees. "Don't. Please. You can't give him money."

Anger spikes through me. How dare she walk into my command room and start giving orders? I sidestep the chair and grab her upper arm. "What are you doing here?"

She addresses the room and not me, acting like I don't even exist. "If he has more money, he can buy and sell more women and children. If you knew what he does to them, what they go through...don't give his family anything. I'll help if I need to. Use me as bait. He'll love a chance to get me back."

I wrap my fingers around her chin and force her to look at me. "Bedroom. Now," I grit out.

She stares me down for a second, and I think I might have to sling her over my shoulder and drag her out. But then she turns, tugs her arm from my grip, and leaves the room.

"You have my orders," I tell Kai. He nods, and I follow her out.

In the hall, she hasn't gone far, and I catch up to her. "What the hell were you thinking? You are the one who came to me to kill that bastard, and now you don't like the way I do it? You don't have a choice, Angel."

She lets out a long sob and then sinks to the floor at my feet. I hate the sight of her bare legs on the cold hardwood, but I crouch down beside her anyway. "What's going on? Tell me, please, before I have to punish you, and neither of us wants that."

She gasps and looks up at me through tear-dotted lashes. "P-P-Punish me?"

"You just walked into my command room, countermanded an order I made to my team, and disrespected me in front of them. What would your father do to you if you had done that?"

Her already pale skin turns ashen. "I just can't let you give him money. More children will be hurt in the most terrible ways. He used to force me to watch videos he and his men made of..." She puts her hand across her mouth and swallows hard like she is about to be sick.

I tuck her head against my chest. It's an awkward angle, but I need to feel her to step back from some of this rage. From the demand to claim and conquer at all costs.

"Talk to me, Angel. Talk to me so I don't do something we'll both regret later."

She wraps her hands around my biceps and lets me hold her tighter. "Wh-hat should I say?"

"Anything, Angel. Anything."

I hear her hard swallow, and then she shifts her head slightly. But she doesn't speak. When she opens her mouth again, she starts to sing an old Czech lullaby, and her voice is...haunting. Not in a please stop singing sort of way. It echoes inside me straight to my memory, and suddenly, it's not my angel and me, but my mother holding me, singing the same lilting song to lull me to sleep.

It sinks into my bones, instantly calming me in a way I haven't felt since I was a child. I still and let her soothe away some of the chaos and some of the darkness.

I pick her up in my arms as she keeps singing to me and carry her back to our bedroom. It's not until I set her on the bed that she stops, and I sink to my knees in front of her. She doesn't make a sound when I spread my shirt open to reveal her bare skin and the tiny lace scrap of her underwear.

If I can't take her, right here, right now, then I'm going to touch her this way. Give her back some of the bliss she's given me.

I strip her panties away in one smooth motion, and her hands sink into my hair.

"Wait, please, don't."

I pause long enough to look up her body at all her pinky pale skin and the soft peach tips of her nipples. "I'm doing this, Angel. Consider it your punishment. We are moving things forward. I won't sink inside you yet, but this is the payment I require for your interruption."

Her fingers sift through my hair a moment, and I allow her time to think about it. Even if the result will be the same. Giving her time won't change what I'm going to do, but if it gives her comfort, then I'll use these little pauses to my advantage.

The seconds tick by without a word. And when she's come to some sort of decision, she spreads her legs a little bit wider and lays her head back on the bed. Right now, she looks like she's about to go through the world's worst doctor's visit. With a front row view of her pussy, I focus on my task.

She's pink here too, and as I spread her open, she gasps. It makes me chuckle. "I haven't even touched you properly yet, Angel. Wait a moment to be impressed."

Her legs quake around my shoulders, and I reach out and scoop her by the ass to drag her toward me. I laugh again at her little squeal of surprise.

"Relax, love, I'm not going to hurt you. The opposite, in fact."

I don't give her time to shy away. I lean and slide my tongue from the little pucker of her asshole to her clit. Everything in her jolts, and I have to wrap my arms around her thighs to keep her from wiggling away.

I lick her again, this time for me, delving my tongue inside her to get a taste. Heaven. Just like I knew she would be.

Then I lick my way up to her clit in short, flat strokes. When I lathe her clit, she jolts again, her fingers finally moving in my hair again.

"Oh, you like that?" I whisper against her wet skin. I suck her clit between my lips and enjoy the way she reacts.

I focus on making her squirm harder in my hold. It's not gentle, me forcing an orgasm on her, but hell, this is supposed to be a punishment.

Her heavy panting reaches me, and I feel her legs tighten around my ears. She's close, and I can't wait to taste the sweet honey of her when she tips over the edge.

It takes seconds for her to fist my hair and arch her back, forcing her pussy harder into my mouth. I give her exactly what she wants and use the tip of my tongue to tease her clit faster.

Her breathy moan as she comes is the sweetest sound I've ever heard. I lick her softer, easing back slowly until she settles on the bed, her hands falling beside her hips.

I give her one more kiss and then stand to look down at her. "And what do you say to me?"

She peeks one eye open and looks at me. "Yeah, that'll teach me."

## 18

## VALENTINA

*E*very time he touches me, I still flinch. I feel bad about it because he has done nothing but pleasure me for the past couple of weeks since his "punishment." Based on what my father would have done to me for butting into things that aren't my business, he could have done a lot worse.

But he's patient with me. Every flinch is met with a kiss and more of his hands on my skin. It's like he can't stop touching me. I guess it's what I made the deal for. I accepted that when we got married, even if I didn't quite understand why he went through all the effort when I'd already signed my life away to him.

I wake up with his fingers between my legs and his mouth on my skin. Some mornings, he rubs himself against me until he comes hot and hard on my thighs. Those times are the hardest to keep from pulling him into my arms and telling him I want all of him.

Some days are easier than others. Most of the time, I'm content with staring at the incredible view from his penthouse or reading a book. It's a lot like being at home without the eggshells I constantly had to walk on. His friends and the guards are courteous, and for the very first time in my life, I feel like I'm actually safe.

I doubt neither my father nor Sal could get to me in this place. They could try, but then they'd face some of the most badass soldiers I've ever seen.

I've convinced myself that if I stay here, inside, then nothing can reach me. Not even my nightmares. Which is a lie and the truth. When he holds me, the world feels quiet, and I feel guilty for grasping onto that feeling and letting it take care of me. Like my happiness is some kind of betrayal to Rose.

On the rare occasion he isn't able to climb into bed beside me, the nightmares come back. I see Sal's face leering and looming over me. I see Rose's eyes accusing me for being the one who survived despite all the things she went through. I see my father's pitying face telling me everything is my fault.

After the nightmares, I wake up in his arms and let him chase away the demons for one more night. I don't know how long I'll be able to outrun them, but I hope when I see proof that Sal is dead, maybe I'll have some peace, maybe Rose will once and for all. Until then, it's a strange ping pong between safety and guilt.

I lie in bed staring at the ceiling. Adrian is already up for the day, long since dressed and gone. When I moved to get up with him, he urged me to stay in bed and relax. My injuries are nothing more than slight aches these days, but he still wants to coddle me. I haven't felt that way since my mother died.

I'm content to stay here as he demands, but I won't dare try to sleep. Not without him beside me.

A rustle comes from the partially open bathroom door. I hate that my first reaction is fear. It crawls along my body, paralyzing me. My senses narrow to watching the door and listening for any other sounds.

The only way to get into the bathroom without walking through the bedroom is to come through the other side from another bedroom. It was apparently supposed to be mine, but Adrian made it clear I was to stay with him, no matter what.

Only me, or him, should be in the bathroom right now. I slowly sit up and creep off the side of the bed. I don't know what I'm feeling. If someone has broken this little piece of safety I've been able to gather around me, I almost feel angry and violent, ready to exact revenge for it.

I carefully make my way across the floor to reach the doorway. Instead of poking my head around the side, I peek through the slit along the hinges. It's not very wide, but it gives me enough of a view to spot anyone in the bathroom.

I don't know what I expect to find, but…Adrian…hips braced against the bathroom counter, his pants around his knees, and his cock in hand is not it.

The background noise washes away as I watch him, intent on seeing him completely stripped of the authority, of his demands, of everything that makes him so fascinating to me.

I still like him. I still want him, even more so as I witness such an unguarded moment. He strokes his hand from base to tip in long slow strokes. I'm curious why he didn't come into the bedroom and ask me to touch him. He's been on edge while I've been trying to acquaint myself with our new intimate relationship, so maybe he just needed to take the edge off.

I'm entranced as he guides his hand up his length and then back down. When his strokes increase in tempo, I lean closer to the door. So close I can hear my ragged breathing bouncing off the wood to reach me.

When he dips his other hand down to cup his balls, I freeze, holding my breath now so I don't miss a single sound he might let slip out.

He's beautiful like this. His thighs thick and muscular, his arms working hard to pleasure himself. A hot coil of need swirls through me. It's a feeling I've only recently started to recognize. But now, it blazes through me full force as I watch him.

Wearing only a white T-shirt and his underwear, I slide my hand down my belly and into my panties as I watch. I clamp my lips tight so he doesn't catch the whimper that escapes me when my fingers reach my clit.

I barely start moving when he lets out a long grunt that shoots right through me. He comes hard, with one hand around the tip to catch his cum and the other working himself fast.

When he starts to wash his hands, I rush back to the bed, climbing onto the covers just in time for him to come out of the bathroom and wipe his hands on a towel. "Awake, Angel?"

I look at him and nod. My body still hot and needy. This ache that seems to bloom when he touches me and never quite lets go.

He stops at the side of the bed and studies me. "Are you going to come eat some breakfast?"

I shake my head. "I'm not very hungry right now. I'll just grab some lunch when I feel like it."

Gently, he slides onto the bed next to me. "What's going on?"

Oh, man. Now I need to pretend I wasn't just watching him while I touched myself. I've never been a good liar. "Nothing."

The tiniest smile curves at the corner of his lips. "Val, your nipples are about to poke through that shirt. And I recognize that pink flush to your cheeks."

I shrug. But he won't let me get away with that.

He snatches my hand so fast I can't even react. When I squeeze my thighs together in an attempt to stifle the ache, his eyes narrow. "What have you been doing up here without me?"

If he takes me touching myself as a sign that I'm ready to go further, to finally consummate things, I don't know if I have the fortitude to turn him away. Yet some part of me knows I'm still scared to go there. Will he force me? It seems unkind to think it, but I can't help it after everything that's happened.

He watches me as he brings my hand up to his lips. I gasp when he sucks my middle and index finger into his mouth and swirls his tongue around them. Then he gently releases my wrist back on the bed and gives me a scorching look. "Did you just touch yourself?"

Since he already knows the answer, I can only nod.

"Were you being naughty and touching yourself while you watched me in the bathroom?"

Again, I nod, a wash of heat hitting my cheeks hard. No doubt even my ears are pink from the blush.

"Show me what you did, where you stood."

His demand is strange, but he's not asking for something I can't give him. I ease off the other side of the bed and go to stand at the doorway of the bathroom to peer along the hinges. I have to reposition the door from where he'd opened it.

"Ah," he says into my ear, and I jump because I didn't even hear him approach. "Did you touch yourself here, or when you were back on the bed?"

"Here," I whisper, not trusting my voice.

He picks me up and carries me back to the bed, bridal style, and lays me on the pillows. This is it. He's tired of waiting, and now that I've initiated something, he'll feel the need to finish it.

"Why do you look so scared right now?"

I shake my head, throwing my chin higher. "I'm not scared."

He slips off his shoes and climbs into the bed. When he crawls up between my knees and gestures at me to open my thighs, I do. I'm trembling as he opens his belt and then his fly and settles between my hips.

"I should punish you, Angel."

I remember our last punishment and get hot all over again. Even with him pressing me into the soft mattress.

"Your pleasure belongs to me and no one else. Not even you. If you need a release, you come to me, and I'll give it to you."

I swallow hard and meet his eyes. "You didn't." While my words are challenging, my tone is barely above a whisper.

He leans in and nibbles at my earlobe, my very, very sensitive earlobe. "And when I've been inside you, and my pleasure belongs to you and you alone, I'll come to you with my needs. Right now, I'm trying to be patient, but smelling your sweet cunt on your fingers isn't helping my control, Angel."

His words are so filthy. I get so turned on every time he speaks to me this way. It makes me wonder if something is wrong with me.

I can feel the hard length of him pressed right over my panties. Exactly where I'm craving him. But it's still terrifying. Will he rip my underwear off and tie me to the bed? Will he force himself inside me? Scenes and images crash into each other inside my head, drawing me from the edge of need and into a whirlwind of panic.

He gently takes my shirt off, and I don't help, staying rigid underneath him. Then he studies my face as he shifts off me and strips my panties away too. He's still wearing clothes, minus his open pants, and now I'm naked underneath him.

My heartbeat is pounding in my ears, and it's not desire coursing through me. I swallow hard and meet his eyes, hoping he's gentle when he does it. If he's easy, soft, then I might be okay. This is the least I can do for him after everything he's done for me. After all, I knew it was part of our agreement.

"Breathe for me."

I blink up at him and realize he's speaking to me.

"Breathe, Valentina, breathe."

I do as I'm told, maybe out of sheer habit. Once the room stops spinning, he's still over me, but he's not doing anything but lying on top of me.

"Want to know a secret?"

I nod, anything to take my mind from the fear.

"I knew you were standing there watching me. I heard you."

## 19

## ADRIAN

Every time she stiffens at my touch, I try to be patient and understanding, but I hate the haunted look she gets in her eyes. I hate how that bastard hurt her and that he is still drawing breath on this planet.

"What's wrong?" I whisper. It's the only thing I can do to keep from yelling and raging. My rational mind knows this is a reaction to her trauma. And the fact she has let me in so far in the couple of months she's been here is amazing. *Patience*, I remind myself for the hundredth time.

"Nothing," she says, but even now, I see she's close to tears.

"Do you think I'm going to hurt you?"

A sob escapes, and she clamps a hand over her mouth. When she gains control of herself, she shakes her head hard. "No, it's not that I think you're going to hurt me. It's just I can't stop the what-ifs from spiraling in my mind. What if you force me down and have sex with me? What if you tie me to the bed? What if—?"

I cut her off with a gentle kiss. "What if I strip you naked and lay on top of you just so I can feel your soft, pretty skin? What if I just like to look at how you flush when you're turned on? What if I want to give you pleasure and take none for myself? How often do the good possibilities squeeze in with the bad?"

"Never. Are you mad?" Her chin is tucked against her chest as if she expects me to strike out at her.

"Angel. I'm not mad. I'm disappointed that I can't help you get past this faster. I'm disappointed I'm not inside you right now. But I would never hurt you. Not ever. I wish you could believe me and know it in your heart."

She glances away, but not before I see the guilt stamped in her eyes and along the rigid line of her eyebrows. "I'm sorry."

"Don't be sorry, just keep trying for me. I'm going to take my clothes off and put myself right back here between your soft thighs. Do you trust me not to enter your body without your permission?"

It takes a few moments, but finally, she nods.

I quickly shift off the bed and strip out of my clothes, leaving them in a pile on the floor. She twitches like she wants to close her legs as I maneuver back between them. I'm already hard again just from looking at her and tasting her arousal on her fingers.

I lie on top of her, bracing my weight onto my forearms so I don't crush her chest. "How do you feel?"

She nods once. "I think okay."

My cock is flush with her pussy, and it would only take the barest of movement to slide into her wet heat. But I won't do it. Not if it means crushing the little bit of trust I've gained over the past couple of months.

"I'm going to keep touching you, all right? But again, I won't push inside you. Nod so I know you understand me."

She does, watching me closely, waiting for every twitch.

I start slowly, leaning in to gently brush my lips with her own. It's easy to kiss her. She's so yielding and soft. Every little whimper she makes for more drives me wild. I deepen the kiss until she touches her tongue to the seam of my mouth for more. Then I give her everything, letting her wind her arms around my neck as I tease her tongue with mine. When I lift my mouth away from hers, she's breathing faster, and her eyes are glazed. This is the way I want my wife, sweet and ready for me to take her. Not scared and ready to bolt.

"What else shall we do?"

The panic enters her eyes again, and I keep my growl of frustration inside. "I told you I won't hurt you, Angel, and I'll keep saying it until you believe it."

She nods again, this time faster as if trying to appease me. I tilt to the side and kiss a trail down her neck. Every inch from her ears to her nipples is so sensitive, and she reacts to the lightest of touches. I alternate kisses, licks, and nibble from her collarbone down to the tops of her breasts. She's panting again and lifting her hips toward me in invitation. If I were a weaker man, I'd take her up on it.

I lean down so I can line my mouth up with her earlobe, then I take a second to enjoy her squirm while I bite down on it. "I want to slide inside you so badly right now. Relax, Angel, I won't do it. This is fantasy. Play with me."

She wraps her arms around my waist, and I love the way her nails feel running down my back.

"Imagine it, think about it...how much pleasure I give you with my tongue. You writhe against my mouth, your fingers tangling with my hair. If I pushed into your wet little channel, I'd make you come in a few short pumps. It's nothing like you've ever felt before."

She whimpers, and I ease my hips forward the tiniest bit so the head of my dick slides across her clit.

Her gasp is enough to bolster me to keep going. "Once I'm inside you, I'll take my time, pulling in and out of you to make you so wet it's dripping out of you down my shaft. I want you soaked for me."

I close my eyes to gain some control over myself. She's not the only one who's turned on right now. It would take seconds to ruin what I've built, and I don't make mistakes.

"What else?" she tentatively whispers. My heart lurches in my chest at her tiny question. Maybe, maybe we can get through this and start our family together.

"Are you aware of how imaginative people are? There are so many positions I want to take you in. I can see your hips in the air, those glorious curls spilled all over the sheets while I pump into your ass."

Her entire body jolts beneath me so hard it makes me pause and meet her eyes. "Okay, Angel?"

She nods again, frantically now. Something tells me that declaration didn't scare her. It excited her. "Do you like your ass played with? I'll have to remember that. When I'm inside you, I can stick my finger or a toy up there and see if you enjoy it."

That earns me another whimper, so I gently ease my hips forward again to slide through the wetness already coating me.

"I'm not done with you yet, though. I want to fuck your mouth so badly. Put my hands in your hair and watch you swallow me down greedily." I have to stop and breathe after that one, my body rigid, my cock so hard it aches.

This time, she meets me in the middle, easing her hips up as I slide along the seam of her pussy. It feels so good, and not just the sensation, but her reacting to me, enjoying herself, and participating.

"But you know what I can't wait for most?"

She squeezes her eyes tight and shakes her head.

"I can't wait to make love to you. Ease you open, slip inside you, and gently show you how sex can be when two people are on the same page. I want to kiss every inch I can reach, and while you're clinging to me, I'll take my time with your body so that when we are done, you won't ever think about anyone else."

"I don't want to think about anyone else."

Her words hit me, making my hips surge up of their own volition. "Say it again," I whisper against her wet lips. "Tell me again."

"I don't want anyone but you. No one makes me feel like this."

I ease forward and back, increasing my tempo the tiniest bit. "Like what?"

"Safe. Cared for. Precious."

I kiss her hard and draw her tongue into my mouth to suck on the tip. She breaks away with a gasp, staring up at me wide-eyed.

"You are precious to me, Angel. Please don't doubt that."

She nods, and I give her a little more sensation, nudging her clit with the head of my cock over and over. With how sensitive she is, I'm surprised she hasn't come already. I'm on the edge of bursting, but not before she does.

"Let's see what else I have in mind for you…I want to take you against the window of our bedroom with the curtains open. No one can see inside through the tempered glass. I'd rip anyone's heart out who tried, but I want to imagine they can, and that they covet you. That they want you for themselves yet will never have you."

She moans this time, again arching her hips up to meet my forward glide.

"You like that too, naughty girl. I can't wait to see what else turns you on. I'm here as you explore what you like, and I can't wait to witness it."

She peers up at me, a softness in her eyes, as her fingers wind up my neck and into my hair. "What do you like?"

I blink, taken aback by her question. But I have to ignore the hollow hole in my chest because she'll never fully be able to give it to me. "You don't want to know."

"Tell me. I wouldn't have asked if not."

I stare down at her and decide to tell her the truth. Lying won't help anything, and she'll learn eventually.

"Pain," I say, matter-of-factly. "When I come, I like to feel pain."

"But not give it?" Her question is barely a whisper.

I gently nuzzle her nose with my own. "Only if the other person wants it."

A part of me wants to remind her, yet again, that I won't hurt her, but I don't. Not with her body so soft and wet underneath me.

I tip forward again, increasing the pace, letting the pressure build. She's so expressive. I can tell she's on the edge of orgasm, and I want to take her over with me.

I move faster, my words stuck in my throat now, because I just want to focus on making her feel good. She's matching me stroke for stroke with her own hips, and I fucking love it.

"That's it, Angel. Come for me. I want to feel you soak me."

She moans, her fingers still tucked tight in the hair at the nape of my neck. Then she tightens her grip, pulling the strands hard enough to send a bolt of pain through me.

"Fuck," I whisper, burying my head in the crook of her neck as I move my hips faster and harder against her. It's not quite fucking, but it feels good enough to sate me. She yanks on my hair one more time, and I don't last. Cum shoots out of me, making things even more wet and slippery.

She's panting and writhing beneath me, and I'm focusing on riding out my orgasm while not sinking deep inside her when it would be so very easy right now. One little angle change and I could feel her heat clasp around me as she comes.

She slowly loosens the grip her body has made around mine. I didn't even realize she'd wound her legs around my ass, and thighs along my hips. Her arms up so she could grip my hair and neck.

I give one long, lingering stroke, enjoying the way my cum makes us slide together so smoothly. "Are you okay, Angel?"

She nods, her eyes sleepy. "Fine. Thank you."

I ease off her and head to the bathroom for a towel. Once we are both clean, I gather her into my arms and snuggle her close into my chest.

One step at a time, I'll win her trust, and then I'll win her heart.

## 20

## VALENTINA

It's been two days since he laid himself on top of me, and I wanted all the things I protested. He could have entered me at any time, but he kept to his word and treated me gently. I don't know why it shocks me every time he treats me kindly. It also wars with all the things Rose told me about him being a monster. However, I guess I haven't been witness to that side of him yet. A part of me hopes I never will.

I stay in bed until the cook calls the room phone to ask if I'm eating breakfast. Once I tell her not to worry about me, I get out of bed, shower, and get dressed. Adrian filled an entire closet for me. Everything is beautiful and in my size. However, staring at some of the pieces, I think he means to take me out of his house, and I'm not sure how I feel about that prospect yet.

I grab a soft white cotton dress that reminds me of summer picnics and slip it on. There are shoes, but I don't bother since I'm staying inside. Then I check my hair in the mirror. Usually I put it up, restrain its heft in some kind of way, but I know how much he loves to touch it, so I leave it down to bounce around my shoulders with a mind of its own.

Since the fiasco in his command room, I usually only come out of the room for meals or to steal a quick book from the shelves tucked in his office. He doesn't have a full library, but I'm wondering if I can change that.

I'm thinking as I walk and completely fail to notice and run smack into an entire hulking person. Solid arms go around me as I stumble, but they aren't Adrian's, and I rip myself free, ready to run. Kai, Adrian's second in command, stands there grinning down at me. I saw him at the party, I thought, and in the command room. He has a distinct air of frivolity to him, from his expensive clothes to the playful grin on his full lips.

"Are you all right? Did I hurt you?" he asks gently like I'm a feral cat ready to strike.

I settle myself and try to be a normal human for once. It's hard when I know he was there that night. That he saw me…"I'm fine. Thank you."

He eyes me carefully, but there's no heat there, not like when Adrian looks me over. I blush all the same, my ears burning. "No, really. I was just looking for Adrian. If he's working, I can go back to my room and wait, though. I don't want to interrupt."

Kai steps to the side and waves his arm gallantly. "I think he's in the dining room. Do you want me to walk with you?"

Shit. What do I say to that? He's just trying to be nice, courteous, to his boss's new pet. So I nod and march past him. He catches up with me, eating the distance with his long legs. He's tall, I only just realized, as tall as Adrian, but not quite as large…he doesn't take up the same kind of space Adrian does.

It hits me that I'm staring, and I focus my eyes back on the hallway again. "Um…so how long have you worked for him?" It sounds dumb even to my ears, I've never been good at small talk, considering my father never let me go anywhere.

"Long enough," he says, with a little chuckle. "We've all been with him a while. You should know, any one of us will keep you safe. He's made sure it's a priority for everyone. You come first."

I blink up at him in surprise. "Me? But why? I'm just a deal he made… Does he usually get so protective about his…?" I can't say possessions, so I just leave it there.

"He's never had a woman here, living with us, staying in his home. I can promise you that."

I don't know why this makes my chest feel tight and my head feel bubbly. "Oh."

When he grins down at me again, I pretend not to notice and keep walking. We get to the dining room doors, and he grips the knob to open it for me.

"Thank you," I whisper and duck inside, closing the door quickly behind me. I've never been good at small talk. Rose has always been my buffer. She was smart, and clever, and cared way too much that everyone adored me the same way she did.

It takes me a second to get a hold of my emotions. The sense of loss I feel threatens to push in on me and drag me to my knees.

"Angel?" Just like that, his voice cuts through the darkness, and I stumble toward him.

He turns in the chair and scoops me into his arms, placing me on his lap. "What are you doing here?"

His tone is even and soft. I can't tell if he is angry or annoyed, which worries me. I can always read people; it's how I've stayed alive through years of abuse. Often, I can just gauge things by how a room feels.

"I just wanted to see you, I guess." It sounds ridiculous, but it's the truth, so I don't try to take it back.

He grabs something from the plate behind me and brings it to my lips. "Eat, Val, you need to eat more. I want you strong and healthy."

I chew on the bit of bacon and swallow, content to let him feed me. It feels nice to be pampered and cared for, and he doesn't seem tired of doing it.

"What are you up to?" I ask after I finish chewing.

He pops the rest of the bacon in his own mouth. "Eating, obviously."

I roll my eyes and shake my head. "After you eat, obviously," I mimic his tone and earn a sharp pinch to my ass.

"I have some things to go over with Kai. Then we need to break up the assignments for my men for the week."

I'm curious about his life, about his business. The society isn't exactly involved in legal activities, but I don't know anything about what he does or doesn't do. "What kind of assignments?"

He nuzzles my neck, peppering kisses around like a collar. "Nothing you need to worry about."

His comment stings. Does he think I'm too stupid to understand? Or that I'm a pampered princess who can't be bothered with the day-to-day life of working people? Of course, I don't say either of these things. I just hug his head to me while he continues his path of kisses.

"Why do you ask?" he says, pulling back to meet my eyes.

But I can't meet his gaze. "No reason. I was just curious." It would be so simple to tell him that I want to be a part of his world and not just an observer. I want to know how he spends his time when he's not with me. I want to know his people can keep him and me safe. I could say all of these things, and once upon a time, I would have. Now, I feel like every conversation could be a minefield.

He watches me closely, and I'm not sure believes me. Another zing of hurt washes through me at that even though he'd be correct.

"You smell different today, what is that?"

I rub the center of my chest. "Sorry, it was in the bathroom. I think it's lavender oil? The bottle said it was good for headaches, but it also smelled nice, so I used it as perfume."

His forehead bunches up and a haunted look enters his eyes. It comes on so fast I cup his cheeks with my hands to look at him. "What? What is it? Are you okay?"

The abject sorrow is gone as fast as it washed over him, and I worry, still scanning his features for any clues.

"It just reminds me of my mother. She used to wear lavender oil. I remember she always smells like this."

Oh, no. I move to climb off his lap, but he captures me against him, not letting me leave.

"I'm so sorry, I didn't know," I say, still trying to get away even as his hold tightens on me.

"No, it's okay. The scent just surprised me. It's fine, really."

I'm still terrified he is about to fling me in the hallway and find someone to shove me out the door.

"Stop fighting me, and be still," he grouses.

I freeze and let him pull me back against his chest. He picks up a bit of toast and presses it to my lips. Obediently, I take it and chew as he watches me closely. Once I finish, he eats the other piece, still content to sit and stare.

The curiosity gets the better of me until I can't hold it in any longer. "What happened to your mother?"

He stills, his entire body just not moving. Shit. I once again prepare myself to run if necessary. Not that it would help me if he wanted to catch me.

"She died a long time ago." His words are soft and filled with so much pain.

I cup his cheeks again and swing my leg over to straddle his lap and get closer. "I'm so sorry. How did it happen?"

He gives me a rueful shrug. "I don't know. Family mystery. Even my bastard father couldn't tell me before he died." Something hard enters his eyes, and I remember. My father is the one who was supposed to have killed Adrian's father. Shit.

"Does anyone else know what happened? Do you want me to contact people on my father's team? They might talk to me."

Or they might tell my father where I am so he sends a lot of guns to get me. I leave that part out.

"No, if there was information to be had, I would already have it. I've been hunting for answers most of my life. I've accepted that I'm just never going to know the truth."

I stroke his hair, careful not to mess it up. "Were you two close?"

"Yes, she was a wonderful woman, and I loved her." A soft smile curls his lips. "She used to wear this bright red scarf. Wool. And it was so old and ragged that bits of it were clumped together and knotted. She loved that thing so much. I remember thinking, when I was a boy, I hoped that one day I would find something I love as much as my mother loved that scarf."

I smile at his memory. A sweet one to share with me. My chest feels tight with the knowledge of it. "That is lovely. She sounds like an amazing person. I wish I could have met her."

He nods once. It's a curt acknowledgment of my sympathy but gives nothing else. "If I have to speak to my father, I'm happy to ask him for you. See if he will tell me what happened. I doubt he would, though. After my own mother's death, he was never the same man. He turned cruel and hateful overnight."

He hugs me tight to him, and I bury my face in the center of his shirt. The scent of him eases me as it always does. I close my eyes and picture a knotted-up worn wool scarf in my head, but the fantasy shifts to a memory as the image of a scarf like that is framed in a pool of blood.

I shake it off, like I shake off most of the bad memories that threaten me these days and focus on the door behind me. It takes seconds to count the squares in the wood. Then I count them again to steady myself one more time and wonder why I can't shake the image all the way.

## 21

## ADRIAN

Two days later, sitting in the same seat at the dining room table, I can't believe I told her about my mother. She's never been someone I talk about with anyone, not even Kai. Yet my angel crawled in my lap and asked me a question, and I poured out all my carefully guarded details.

I focus on Valentina. She joined me for breakfast today. Her hair was held out of her face by some pins, and a soft pink dress hugged her biteable curves. That cotton would feel nice around my shoulders as I put my mouth on her.

The urge to pick her up, put her on the table, and drop to my knees is also overwhelming. Would she let me do it or try to push me away? Would she be free with her reactions like she is in bed or try to curb them in case anyone outside the room was listening? She sits a foot away reading a newspaper, and I can only think about how wet she gets when I tongue her and each little sound she makes as she comes.

I shift in the chair and rearrange my hard-on, which had been pressing into the edge of the table. She doesn't even look up from her reading. It's adorable how focused she can get. The rest of the world doesn't exist for her right now. It's a skill I envy because the outside world is all too real for me every second of every day. The only time it gets quiet is when I'm touching her.

The door bursts open, and Alexei stalks into the room. He's all tall, lean muscles, dark hair, and leather. This gets her attention, and I have to remember she's mine, and Alexei wouldn't dare touch her. His gaze rests on me, waiting.

"What is it?" I'm irritated, and my tone shows it, but he seems unfazed.

"There's news. You should come to the command room." Message delivered, he lopes back out of the room. If the man wasn't the best sniper I'd ever seen, I'd be concerned about his skills at first glance.

I look up at Valentina, and she's watching me, not even trying to hide her curiosity. When I smile, she absent-mindedly smiles back. "Stay here or go to our room. I'll find you when I'm finished."

She blinks a couple of times, nods, then turns back to her reading. An English muffin in one hand, the page of the newspaper in the other.

If he hadn't barged in, I would have put her on the table and tested out the fantasies in my head. Alexei always did have terrible timing and zero tact.

I entered the command room to find the whole team sitting around the table once again. Andrea's black boots are propped on the edge. Kai is perfectly quaffed next to my favorite chair. Alexei is slumped into the chair next to his twin. Vincent, Ivan, and Michael ring the other side of the table to my right.

But Kai is the one who delivers the news. "Valentina's father has returned home."

An image of the old man walking into the house with a suitcase dragging behind him comes up on the screen.

"Anything else," I wave impatiently.

Kai loads up some more images and lays them all out on the big monitor. Nothing indicates Sal is with him or that he's been there since the night he attacked Valentina.

"The staff who have pretty much been MIA since we rescued her have all suddenly gone back to work today."

I sit back and study the images. "Well, it'll make things easier for us to question them too. We need someone in there."

Kai nods. "I have someone already. I trust them to report back."

He's never steered me wrong yet, so I nod, content to let him figure those things out. "And Sal, has he shown his face yet? I don't see him in any of these images."

Kai grins, a dimple popping on his cheek. "That's where things start to get fun. We bugged his office some time ago, and the old man is so anti-technology that he doesn't bother to sweep for things like that. Anyway, we overheard him talking on the phone to Sal's family. He laid down some threats, demanding his daughter be returned to him, untouched."

I grimace. We can all guess what he means by untouched, and it disturbs me that her father is concerned with it. But if it's the only reason Sal hadn't finished things with her, I suppose I should be thankful.

"Any eyes or ears at his family's estate? What about the deal we offered? Any word on their response?"

Kai's smile slips, and I glance around the table as every one of my fearless men avoids eye contact. "What is it?"

"They sent some pretty nasty words thinking that we were somehow laying a trap for them or Sal. I don't know if they are aware of what their son did to Valentina, but they don't seem inclined to entertain any kind of deal during the season."

It was a long shot anyway. I didn't expect them to accept, especially not on the first offer. The season is always a tumultuous time. Empires rise and fall in a few short months, and I hope by the end of this one, Valentina's father's house will be destroyed. But only a few weeks remain to complete the work, and one final party where I plan to make an entrance.

"Send one more offer. If they are rude, send them a little gift to let them know we don't appreciate our kindness being rebuffed. Maybe that will inspire them. I'm tempted to put a ridiculous price on Sal's head and send it out to all the families. His isn't the only family hard up for money."

Kai considers and shakes his head. "I'd wait, boss. The season is almost over, and you know that once things lock down, any activity will be considered an act of war against the council."

"Thanks for the society lesson," I quip, still studying the images. "What else did her father say to Sal's family? Anything about me?"

"Nope, not a mention. Not even the staff have discussed you. We've been monitoring the few we saw the night we breached the house and took her out. They seem too scared to discuss it or possibly to be the messenger her father kills when they deliver the bad news. He may be old, but he can lift a gun just fine."

I'm happy there hasn't been mention of my name yet. I want my involvement secret until I choose to reveal myself and my actions. More than anything, I want to see the look on that old bastard's face when he sees I've taken his only bargaining chip. He's circling the drain, and he's too damn stubborn to give up with some dignity. That's fine by me. I don't plan to offer him any.

"Make sure our offers to Sal's family stay private for now. If any of them mentions it to outside parties, deal with it. We keep things under wraps until I decide it's time to reveal Valentina as my wife to society."

Kai swipes the screen, and the pictures disappear.

"Keep eyes on him. I want to know everything he does and everything he says."

"Of course."

Everyone else is quiet as I glance around the table. "Do you have anything else for me to handle right now?"

They all shake their heads, and I nod. Kai can handle what they need for any of his tasks. No one comes to me for anything these days anyway.

I turn to face Kai. "What are the odds the old man takes out Sal for us? As interesting as that dynamic could be, I don't want to lose my chance to rip that slimy weasel apart piece by piece. I want him to know exactly what I took from him and exactly what he gave up for his twisted games."

"I don't think he would kill him unless he had definitive proof Sal did something to Valentina. Right now, he's just spouting off about Sal taking her to marry off without doing things properly."

It went to show how much he knew about his own business partner and daughter's fiancé. Sal would never steal Val away to marry her. To rape her, absolutely, but never to marry her when he can do that legitimately and get all the money he thinks is coming to him.

"Well, monitor things and make sure. The old man might know a special place Sal likes to hide out. Follow him to see if he makes any moves, especially to places we've logged as possible hideouts."

A hush goes around the room again, and I meet each of their eyes. "What? What the fuck are you all staring at?"

Alexei breaks the awkward silence. "Andrea wants to know if you've taken the princess to bed yet."

Kai drops his head, shaking it over the table, but I can't tell if he's ashamed or he's laughing. If anyone else asked me such a question, I might put a bullet in their head after I made them apologize to my feet. These men earned the right to question me, so for them, I simply flip them off and focus on Kai. "They obviously need more to do if they are worried about my sex life."

I shoot a look at Alexei. "Also, don't fucking call her princess."

He gives me a clipped nod and then elbows his sister, who is grinning from ear to ear. I flip her off individually just to make sure my point is made.

"Keep all our current surveillance in place. Get some people into Sal's current businesses so they can be monitored at all times. I want him, and I want him alive so I can change that. Understood?" My tone is sharper than usual, but no one seems disturbed by it.

I settle back into the chair and wave at the screen. "Bring up the images again. I want to get a look at him. We still need to find out why he was out of town that long. Business deals don't take that much time, but other things do." My brain is headed down a track so fast it takes a moment for me to catch up. "Medical procedures would take that long. Start checking hospital records. Bribe, steal, whatever you need to do to track down the information."

It gives me a little thrill to think the old man is finally getting what he deserves. If he is sick, I hope it's brutal and eats him from the inside out.

"Anything else?"

Kai shakes his head while everyone else sits and waits for me to leave. I push out of the chair and head out. These assholes. They've earned my respect, my friendship, and my disgruntlement. It happens regularly, but this time, I want to bang heads together because they were talking about Valentina.

While my brain ran off that well-worn track, something else occurred to me. If I don't find Sal soon, will Valentina decide our contract is unfulfilled and try to leave? It's not as if I'll let her walk out the door. She is my wife, after all, but if she took the contract to the council and showed it unfulfilled, they could grant her asylum and help her dissolve our marriage.

White-hot rage pours through me at the idea. There isn't a person alive who could take her from me. Some part of me wants them to try so I can set the example of what happens if anyone does.

The anger eats at me while I head to my office and slam the door behind me. Let them think I'm mad at them for now. My head is spinning because I need to find Sal. I won't give her a reason to walk away.

## 22

## VALENTINA

I'm in bed before Adrian comes in for the night. We saw each other at dinner for a moment, but then he had to go off and handle some business meetings. The season is about to end, and it hits me how much has changed since I attended the first party. It feels like so long ago that I was excited about going to my first society event. Now, it's all so hollow. As if I would see that girl and tell her to stop being a moony idiot. Since then, I've learned my world is so much darker than I'd ever imagined. And somehow, the man who is supposed to be the darkest star has become my light.

It's these thoughts chasing through my head as he closes the door behind him. I watch as he crossed the room, removing his jacket and slipping off his shoes. It's a graceful dance he's done every night, and it's never any less mesmerizing.

His shirt comes next, his wide shoulders flexing as he strips it off and tosses it on an armchair near his closet. When he gets to his belt, the book I held in my lap is already forgotten, and I can't keep my eyes off him. I don't know if he realizes I watch him so closely or not. I really don't care if he does. I like to look at him, and he doesn't bother hiding his own interest when he watches me dress or undress.

"I can feel your eyes drilling holes into my back, Angel," he says as he takes off his watch and places it gently on the dresser. Guess he answered that question.

When he turns to face me, he's only wearing tight black boxer briefs. His abs are outlined all the way up to his solid pecs, and I can't take my eyes from him.

"You're staring," he says, but there's an affectionate lilt to his tone that makes me offer a sheepish smile.

"I could say I'm sorry, but I don't think I am."

He dives toward the bed and slides in alongside me. In seconds, I'm dragged into his arms. "Where did that smart mouth come from? I'll have to put it to use if you've got nothing better to do than give me attitude."

"You watch me too." I feel the need to point out. To defend myself.

"So I do," he says, dropping his mouth to the upper curve of my breasts to bite gently.

I arch into him, loving the way he feels against me. He's been giving me time, allowing me to come to terms with what I've been through, but right now, sex doesn't seem like a hardship. I've learned he knows how to make it good for me, and I know he won't hurt me any more than necessary.

Maybe I should offer myself to him and just get it over with. It's been such a big deal in my head, but I want to shrink it down and make it meaningless. If it means nothing, then maybe it can't hurt me.

He shifts on the bed to lie on his side and pull me closer. We stare into each other's eyes, and I want to stay here. Just live this tender moment for the rest of my life. If only he'll keep looking at me like that.

"Anything you want to say since you were so focused on my undressing?" he teases.

I shake my head, heat washing into my neck, no doubt staining my chest and face pink above the cream silk of my nightgown. "No. I just enjoy watching you sometimes, is all."

A part of me can't believe I admitted that to him out loud. As if men need more ego stroking than they get on a daily basis. But it's equally important to me for him to know that I think he's beautiful. "You're lovely when you're not on display for anyone."

"Yet you were watching me like I was. How do you know I wasn't performing for you?"

I smile and snuggle closer. "You might have been. If so, I feel special that you would expend so much energy to please me."

He rears back in an inch as if my answer surprises him. "There you go again, disarming me with bold honesty. I like when you do that. It makes me hard."

The straightforward way he tells me about his erection sends heat through my already throbbing body. My heartbeat is in my ears already, but now, I'm warm through and through.

His compliments make me feel a little more confident. Despite the blush burning my ears, I enjoy the fact he finds me sexy. If Sal ever did, he never said it, only offered plenty to say about my frigidity. Not that I cared too much about his opinion. Adrian's, however, I do care about. I want him to look at me and see me as a woman.

I place my hand on his chest and gently push him to lie on his back. He watches me with a sexy little grin on his face. The man doesn't smile much, but when he does, damn, I want to make him keep doing it.

"What are you up to, Angel?" He's amused, and that's fine since any minute now, I'm going to need his help to complete my plan.

Once he's completely flat and shifts in the bedding to flatten his hips, I scoot closer, gently easing one leg over his, and then another so I'm kneeling between his thighs. I can't help but stare at the outline of him, already hard in his underwear.

He's watching me, the amusement gone, replaced by pure fire. "Angel," he prompts. "Don't tease me."

Lifting, I put one leg on either side of his wide solid hips. Somehow, I always forget how huge he is until we get more intimate.

The length of him brushes at my panties, and I settle my hips back, so I press there.

He hisses out a breath and captures the meatiest part of my thighs in his hands. "You want to play games tonight? Or do you want something else?"

I get the gist of sex, but I'm terrified to reach into his underwear, draw him out, and sink onto him. Nor do I have any clue how he would react if I did. "I'm not sure what I should do now," I admit.

He kneads the muscles of my legs gently. "Did you have a plan here? Or were you just winging it?"

I know my face is burning bright pink. "Winging it. I saw you come in and thought…why don't we get this whole sex thing over with."

His face bunches up in a heavy scowl. "Over with? What makes you think sex with me is going to be a one-and-done affair? Especially when I've given you ample evidence to the contrary?"

Okay. True. He's made it clear he wants me in every single way he can get me. I still find myself drifting off to fantasy land when he listed all the things he wanted to do to me while I came.

"I didn't mean it like that. I'm…nervous." It takes a lot for me to tell him this simple truth, even if he can probably see it for himself.

"Why?"

"We haven't done this yet. I'm ready, but I'm not sure at the same time. I want you so much I burn with need, but sometimes, you scare me."

His scowl deepens. "Scare you, how?"

I sigh and slump. "Not like that. Just...I don't know what to do with all of you most of the time."

Another tiny grin lights up his face. "All of me?"

When I don't answer, he lifts his hips, bucking me upward, and twists us over so he now lies in the cradle of my thighs. "All of me?"

"You're a big guy. Solid. Beautiful. I feel like you deserve a woman who can get her full use out of you."

He laughs, throws his head back and laughs so hard I feel it in my toes. When he stops, tears shimmer at the corner of his eyes, but his smile is gone. "I don't want any other woman but you. If you make me tell you again, I'm going to have to come up with another punishment. This one would be less enjoyable than the last."

I nod once to let him know I understand. Is this it? Will we have sex now? I scan his face, waiting for a sign I should be ready; that any moment he's going to fuck me, and I can finally stop worrying about it.

"Tell me what you need, Angel. Didn't I say you should come to me with your needs? Say it out loud, and I'll give you anything."

I feel ashamed, but it doesn't stop me. "I ache when I look at you."

His voice drops to a deeper register, which resonates through me. "Where? Show me."

I grip one of his hands and ease it between our bodies until his fingers lay over my panties at the level of my clit.

"I'm proud of you. I know it's not easy, but you will always tell me when you want me, and I'll make sure you're taken care of."

"What if you're in a meeting? Or out of town?"

He dips his head and nips my chin with his teeth. "If I'm out of town, love, you'll be with me. If I'm in a meeting, well, I'll just have to guide you through what I want to do to you via email or text."

It's time to point out the obvious. "I don't have a phone."

He doesn't respond to that because he's too busy dragging his face down my front, bunching the silk up and away until his lips can touch my bare skin.

"You taste so delicious. Let me feel you come on my tongue."

I don't bother smothering the moan his words inspire. He drags my panties down my legs in one rough jerk. Then he's nudging my thighs apart with his huge shoulders and lowering his face to my pussy.

"Do you want it fast, slow, soft, easy? Tell me what you're in the mood for."

I don't tell him I'm in the mood to feel more than just his mouth. I'll settle for this if it's what he wants. "Fast and hard."

"My favorite," he murmurs against my wet skin. He doesn't bother with niceties, going straight to my clit and sucking it hard.

I delve my fingers into his hair to give me an anchor, so I can watch his hips hump into the bed when I pull the strands hard enough to give him a little edge of pain.

God. How did this happen? I'm addicted to this man and everything he brings out in me.

"Harder," I say.

He only lathes at me harder, sucking, licking, nibbling harder until I'm writhing on the sheets and shoving his face against my body. Not once does he stop or complain. He doesn't lift his lips from my skin until I've stopped shuddering from the strength of my orgasm.

I feel like he's turned me inside out. My arms fall away from his hair, and he crawls up my body, then turns to lie beside me and drag me into his arms.

Curled against his shoulder, I run my hand down his abs, intent on giving him back some of the pleasure he gave me. When I reach his shaft, he stops me and brings my fingers to his lips. "This was for you. I don't need anything in return. Yet."

The tag on seems ominous, but it still starts a new desperate throb under my skin. When will I have enough of him? And how can I rectify everything I've lost with everything I've gained?

## 23

## ADRIAN

She's reading in bed again. Her knees are drawn up, and a book rests in the cradle her thighs make. I watch her for a minute while she's completely oblivious. My wife is so beautiful. Looking at her creates an ache in my chest.

After I've looked my fill, I cross the room and lay a garment bag across the bed. She peers over at me, her eyes bouncing back and forth between me and the bag. "What's that?"

"A dress."

She gives me her best try at a stern look, and it's so fucking adorable. "I have a whole closet of dresses you've bought me. I don't need another."

"This one is special."

When she closes the book, she slips her index finger between the pages as if this conversation won't take long enough for her to properly mark her spot. "Oh?"

I unzip the bag and spread it open to remove the dress. It's black velvet and cut exactly to her measurements. It will fit her like a second skin, and I am already hard thinking about her wearing it.

"Wow, it's beautiful," she breathes. "What's it for?"

"The end of the season party. It's time to take you out and present you as my wife."

My statement throws her. I watch emotions chase across her expressive face as she tries to figure out how she feels. A part of me expects a fight, but after a few seconds, she nods and gives me a soft, "Okay." Then she opens her book again.

My fingers tingle as a surge of adrenaline batters me from the inside. "Does this mean you finally trust me to keep you safe?"

She glances up from the pages. "It's not that I didn't trust you specifically. It's hard for me to trust anyone at all. No matter how much I want to."

"Do you think you can do this for me? Come to the party and stand on my arm, look pretty, and smile."

She makes a face when I say the word *smile,* but then she nods. "It will be hard, but if you're with me, then it might not be so bad. What if my father is there?"

"From our intel, it doesn't look like he's attending, and he didn't RSVP. But if he does show, well, it'll make for an interesting night since he can't do anything to me on neutral ground. Nor can he take you away since you're legally my wife."

"And Sal...?" she barely whispers.

I smile now, and she looks shocked by it. "If Sal shows up, it's going to be an excellent night because I'll finally get to hold up my end of our deal and give you everything I want. He has it coming."

I leave the dress and go to my closet to gather my own clothing. "I'll ask Andrea to come help you get ready."

Her eyes are shimmering with tears, and my heart clenches. I want to comfort her, but she needs to do this. She needs to face these people for herself. And while she does, I'll keep her safe.

I meet Valentina and my team at the elevators when it's time to leave. As usual, she looks stunning. She fidgets with the tiny bag in her hands as if she has no clue what to do with her fingers.

When she reaches me, I lift her chin and stare into her eyes. "You are my wife. You'll be the mother of my children, and you should keep your chin up. No one talks down to you, no one touches you, and no one but my team goes anywhere with you alone. Understood?"

She swallows heavily and then nods. I'm proud of her as she keeps her head high all the way to the car. Once inside, I settle her on the seat next to me, needing to touch her before I have to slip into the mask of society.

"Don't be alarmed if I treat you or anyone else differently while we are at this party. People come to expect certain things from me, and I like to maintain the façade so they don't look deeper."

She lifts her chin to stare up at my face. "I don't like lying."

"You don't have to lie. If they make assumptions about you or me, that's on them. Let them dig their own graves. It makes our lives easier."

A slow shiver moves through her, and I clutch her tighter. "We won't stay any longer than necessary. I have a little business to handle, and then once we've shown our face around the ballroom, we can leave."

The car pulls up outside The Holland Hotel, and Kai opens the passenger door to assist Valentina out. No one will be able to take their eyes off her tonight. She's accented the dress with heavy eye makeup that makes her smolder. Her hair, for once, is straight in a long sheet down to her shoulder blades. Andrea slicked it away from her face, making my little angel look like hell in high heels. I want these people to think she'll eat them alive, and Andrea certainly helped deliver.

We enter the party with Val tucked tight to my arm. My team, also in black, fans out behind us. They've already been briefed that Valentina's safety comes first. Also, if Sal dares show his face, they are to grab him if they can and stash him until we leave.

I scan the partygoers' faces as they stare. Each of them eyes our clothing, and then their eyes bug out as they notice the rings on our fingers, which I made to display prominently. The sooner they all know Valentina's mine, the better. There won't be any misunderstandings that way. I'd hate to break the rules of the hotel for a little misunderstanding.

We reach the bar, and I order her a drink. It'll keep her fingers busy and her ring out for everyone to note. I wish I'd had time to bend her over the bed and mark her pretty skin with my teeth. Give them another reason to talk and her another mark of my ownership.

I don't know why we have this same party every year. The same people, the same location, the same drinks. Death and decay are the only things that make a change in this crowd, which doesn't seem like a reason to celebrate to me. My father used to tell me the end-of-the-season party was a way to start negotiation for alliances since no one can move on other territories out of season…that time is reserved for new partnerships.

There's not a single person here who I'd want to align myself with. No one I can trust except my own men.

Val squeezes my arm, and I do a quick sweep of her head to toe to make sure she's okay. Her face seems a little pale, and her fingers are wrapped tight around my forearm, but otherwise, she doesn't look like she might pass out or run away. Good. I give her a little kiss on the top of her head and make deliberate eye contact with those lingering nearby to get a better look at us.

"I have to go handle some business, Angel. Stay with one of my men, and you'll be all right."

Her eyes go panicky. "Don't leave me alone."

"You'll be with friends. Kai, Andrea, Alexei. They are all right here, prepared to keep you safe. Say the word, and they'll be right here by your side."

Her hands are shaking as she clutches her drink tightly. "But I want you by my side. I can't do this."

I lift her chin and stare into her eyes. "You're a Doubek now, and there's nothing you can't handle. Just make the world think you will tear them apart."

She blinks rapidly as if trying to push away tears and then nods. "Hurry, please."

I slip through the crowd, content that my men have her. They were already circling when I started to walk away. Kai is at my back, following me across the room where I spotted just the man I'd come here to meet.

Nic Diavolo isn't part of this society. He's not even local, but occasionally, he comes in for business, and when he does, he's one of the few people in existence I feel I can trust.

Tonight, he's dressed similarly to everyone else, but his bow tie is undone, along with the buttons at his collar, displaying the tattoos up his neck. Society members give him a wide berth, and they are right to.

I clasp him on the shoulder when I get near. His second in command, Soo, moves through the crowd keeping an eye on us. "After all these years, Soo still doesn't trust me?"

Nic smiles and takes a swig of his drink. "Soo doesn't trust anyone. Why am I here? When I said I had business in the city, I didn't mean I wanted to come to some bullshit party."

"It is a bullshit party, but I had to show my face. This makes it easier since you're leaving early. I need to find this man." I tug a picture out of my pocket of slimy Sal and offer it to him.

He scans it and then passes it back to Soo. "Your men haven't had any luck."

"He's hiding, and it's apparently the only thing the asshole is good at."

I glance over my shoulder, trying to spot Val through the crowd but can't. It grates on me, but I focus on Nic again. "The reward will make the effort worth it. You have my word."

Nic nods, and Soo has already disappeared. "I'll let you know when I have something. The usual payment will suffice, and I expect interest for making me dress up for this circus."

"Seems reasonable. I'm only here tonight to present my wife to society, then we are gone."

A grin splits Nic's face. "Wife, huh? I didn't peg you for the marrying kind."

I slap him on the chest, jostling his drink, but he doesn't care. "You're one to talk. I didn't think you would ever do it either."

He shrugs. "When you know, you know."

I nod, understanding completely. "I need to get back to her. I hate leaving her alone, even with my men around her. Let me know if you find him. Don't kill him, though. That will be my pleasure and no one else's."

Another wicked grin splits Nic's face. He seems quicker to smile now, happier. "Consider it done. Let's chat for a minute, and then I'll let you get back to your wife. Tell me about this target. Soo will do most of the hunting, but I've been known to bring in an asshole or two. If he catches sight of me, he'll piss his pants. I've dealt with his family before, briefly, and only as a last resort to move a shipment. None of them deserve to keep breathing for much longer."

"He took something that didn't belong to him. Before I married my wife, he was her fiancé. She came to me to deal with him, and I haven't been able to do so yet. He's been running since he, well, found out I was looking for him."

No one needed to know what that bastard had done to Val. That would stay between us, and I'd list off every single one of his sins for Sal as I cut him to pieces. In that way, the truth would stay between him and me as well.

Nic isn't the type to press, something I appreciate about him. "Anything else I need to know?"

"Get his phone if he has it. Don't let him destroy it. He might try if he gets caught. I need to check it for any videos he might have taken."

There are questions in Nic's eyes, but he doesn't ask. "Well, then. I'll find him, and I won't be gentle about it. But I won't kill him. Deal?"

I nod, shaking his hand again. "Deal."

## 24

## VALENTINA

The moment the crowd swallows him up, the room starts to close in on me. I take a step backward but bump into Andrea, who easily catches my upper arms and steers me to the edge of the room.

Towering well above me in platform heels, she ducks her head to catch my eyes. "Breathe. If you have a panic attack and die, we'll all be goners a few minutes later."

Her statement shocks a laugh out of me, and I suck in a few breaths through my nose. She nudges my drink to my lips, and I take a sip. "I'm fine. I'm his wife. I can do this."

In my head, I'm giving myself a pep talk, but a tiny voice in the back of my mind tells me it's all an act. He married me to keep me safe. He married me to fulfill a deal. He married me for a pretty play toy spiced up with revenge against my father for my ownership.

It's fine, though. We both get what we want, right? It's not like I'm falling for how safe he makes me feel. Or for the way he wakes things inside me I didn't know existed.

No. I can do this. It's a game. A part he's given me to play, and for my safety, for saving me, I won't let him down.

The problem is as I peer through the crowd, I keep catching sight of Rose. I know she's not real, but all I see is the night of our first party and how she stayed by my side. God, I miss her so much it's like a hole in my chest that won't ever close up. Tears threaten to fall, so I stare up at the ceiling just like she taught me. Never show your weakness. Don't let them see the tears.

When I get control over myself, I give Andrea a nod. "I'm okay, I think."

"Okay. I have to go do surveillance. Kai is close by, so if you need anything, just look at him."

"Go. I'm fine." I nudge her away and face the room with my chin up. Nothing about my insides feels confident, and I wish Adrian were here with me, but it won't be for long, and then we can go.

Another flash of Rose, her eyes, as they were that night, hit me full force, and a wave of nausea threatens my calm act.

I skirt the edge of the ballroom and head to the ladies' room. A hand catches me by the elbow before I can push inside. It's Kai, his eyes asking if I'm okay.

"I'll be out in a moment. I just need a second to collect myself."

The lounge area is made up of seating and mirrors with the restrooms and sinks set back into another area around a corner. I don't bother going all the way through but sink onto a plush navy-blue settee and breathe.

Everything looks the same as the last time I came here when Rose and I were together. I can practically hear her talking to me from the stalls as she pees, like she doesn't have a care in the world. When we both knew that to be a lie. She was good at acting too.

Oh. It's not Rose. Someone is talking to me. I stare up a pair of tan, toned legs to a very short red dress and farther still to long silky white-blond hair. "Are you even listening?"

I blink. "I'm so sorry. I'm in my own little world. Can I help you?"

She narrows her eyes, and the face I thought beautiful only a moment ago turns cold and calculating. "You're pathetic. I don't understand why he would choose you over me." Her Slavic accent is heavy, but the girl is pissed about something.

I stand, mostly because I don't like being towered over, and straighten my dress. "I'm not sure what you're talking about, but excuse me."

She grabs my upper arm hard, her long red fingernails digging into my skin. It would hurt if I hadn't been dished out pain every day of my life. I stare down at her hand and then back up at her face, and something wakes inside me. Something that's slept for far too long.

"Take your fucking hands off me before I break your fingers."

She releases me, but only for a second, as she snatches my left hand in her own. "This ring should be mine. I earned it."

I twist out of her grip, and I want to grab her back, push her as much as she is trying to push me, but I can't. "I don't know what you're talking about, but leave me alone before I call security."

Her face takes on a mottled shade of red, and she steps toward me, leaning down to get right in my face. "You're not worthy, bitch. He's mine. I put up with his bullshit for a long time. He said he would marry me."

"And you are?" I keep myself calm because it's what Adrian would do. I keep my voice level because it's what Rose would do. And I step right up to meet her because I'm tired of assholes pushing me around because they think I'm soft.

She narrows her eyes. "You know who I am. Surely you've heard of me."

I shrug, unconcerned. And I am. Any minute, one of the guards will be in here to check on me, so it doesn't matter if she gets in my face. If she keeps it up and Adrian finds her here, she might not have one afterward, though.

"I have no idea who you are. Now back up before my security details sees you in my face. Obviously, if Adrian wanted to marry you, he would have. But looking at you, I can already tell you're not his type."

Some kind of emotion chases across her features: hurt, denial, a truth she's tried to lie to herself about. Yeah. I bet I'm not the first woman in Adrian's life who's met this woman.

A heartbeat passes, and she resumes her ice queen persona, even giving me a cocky little grin. "Whatever. You'll get what you deserve." She leaves, and I stare at the closing door like I've missed something.

The lock snicks a second later, and I rush over to test the handle. Oh yeah, definitely locked.

An arm snakes around my middle, and a hand curls around my neck. It's a position I've been in multiple times, and the scent of him hits me first. So hard I almost puke up what little alcohol I drank.

"Did you miss me, baby?" Sal hisses in my ear.

I should scream. Now would be a good time to scream, but I can't make any part of my body move at the moment. I can't yell. I can't fight. I can barely breathe.

He tugs me tight into him, and I feel his erection against my lower back. "Don't worry. I asked Olenka to help me get a few moments alone with you. She was eager to meet you and tells me the funniest stories."

His mouth traces down my neck, and he gathers me tighter against him as my legs give out. "Oh, not so fast, baby. Did you give him what you wouldn't give me? I bet he's fucked you in every hole you have, and now, it doesn't matter if you're spoiled for your wedding night. I can take you right here, and no one can do a thing about it."

My cheeks are wet, and a sob rips out of me. Finally, something. I try to shove his hands away, but he tightens his hold, easily lifting me off my feet. The cut of the gown makes it impossible to regain my footing.

He shoves me down onto the settee, front first, and holds my head into the velvet fabric so hard I can't breathe. I flail out, scratching and kicking until he must let me go, and I suck in a gasp of air.

"Oh, don't worry, I'm only getting started. I want to know what Adrian Doubek liked so much that he supposedly married you. Or is it a game he's playing to hurt your father? Maybe he didn't marry you, and he's only keeping you as his hostage and forcing you to pretend." He shoves my face down again. "Tell me he's forcing you. Tell me you didn't agree to marry him when you're supposed to be my wife! Tell me, Valentina."

I fight again, trying to draw in air. Way too many seconds later, he releases his hold on the back of my neck. My hair falls out of its restraints, tangling around my face as pieces stick to my wet cheeks. It's all crystal clear, like my brain wants to latch on to the last few minutes of my life. I have no doubt he's going to rape me, and then he's going to kill me.

I wasn't strong enough to protect Rose or myself when it really mattered. And now, I'm not strong enough yet again, despite Adrian's careful handling of me. His restraint and his patience. I'm going to die in a fucking hotel bathroom because I can't fight my abuser. Rose would be so disappointed in me right now.

And it's like thinking about her conjured her. A soft hand lifts my chin gently, and I see her there, wearing the same too-small dress she wore that night we had fun and played pretend. "Don't let him do this to you. You are so much stronger than this, love. Get up and fight."

Tears pour down my face, and I want to tell her not to go. If she'll just stay with me, we can go together, anywhere she wants. If she'll just stay.

A loud rip pours reality down my spine along with a wash of cold air. He's taking my clothes off.

No. I won't let him do this to me again. Not without some kind of fight, and maybe, Adrian will get here before he can…

I try to hit him with my fists, but he's got leverage and the point of a knife against the back of my neck. So I do the only other thing I can think of. I twist my legs with his and send him sprawling to the floor. It's only seconds, but I fling myself over the edge of the settee toward the door. At the same time, the lock clicks, and someone rushes into me. I cling to them, not even paying attention to who it is.

But then I smell him, and I hear the sharp cadence of his voice, and I sag in relief. Of course, his arms go around me and lift me easily. "Angel. Speak to me. Are you all right?"

"Rose saved me. I'm fine. She saved me."

He clutches me to his chest, and someone drapes a tuxedo jacket over the front of me. All of which was exposed thanks to Sal destroying my dress.

"Get that fucker. Don't let him get away," Adrian says from above me.

I let his words sink into me and comfort me. Even if it's all an act, I don't want to let him go. "Please, don't leave me."

His arms tighten around me. "No one is leaving you, Angel. I'm right here. We're in the elevator going to the car now. Kai and the team are searching for Sal."

"I mean, when you kill him, and we are done with our deal, please don't leave me." I try to open my eyes and look up at him to memorize his face and keep it forever. "When you're done with me, I still want to stay." It's idiotic. What woman in their right mind would want a relationship like that? All give and no take.

But I'll give him every single part of me if he promises to take them.

## 25

## ADRIAN

She's so quiet in the car ride back to the penthouse that I have to keep checking that she's breathing. Holding her, I feel a little less like burning the world down. At the very least, Sal signed his own death warrant by touching Valentina. Not just from me, but by society rules. More than just my team will be hunting for him now. As for Olenka...I gave her to Andrea to play with. No doubt she'll be screaming for mercy within the hour.

Val's dress is ripped—cut—up her back, and I keep moving it to cover her when she or the car shifts. Another wave of white-hot rage rolls through me every time I do. He touched her, hurt her, after I promised her she would be safe. I don't break my promises.

What's worse, for some reason, she thinks the moment I kill Sal that our deal is complete. My careful handling of her feels like it was all for nothing. She expects me to take her as payment for services rendered. If all I wanted was a woman to fuck, there are a hell of a lot less complicated ways to get a bed partner. Hell, I could have had my pick from any society darling, fucking her right there on the ballroom floor, and her family would have still thanked me for choosing her.

Valentina doesn't understand our world as well as I thought she did. Nor does she know me as well as I need her to. It only makes me angrier because the realization hurts. It fucking hurts, and I hate that she has this power now.

She stirs in my arms, and I clutch her tighter. "Rest, Angel. I've got you."

When we reach the penthouse, Kai opens the doors for me all the way up until we are behind my very thorough security. Then I set her gently on her feet and wrap my jacket around her tightly.

It's a stalling tactic so I don't turn and gut every single one of my men. I'm reminding myself that these people are my friends. Yet they almost let my wife be raped and killed in the fucking hotel bathroom.

Kai steps in front of the rest of them, all except Andrea, who is dealing with Olenka. He'll try to take the blame, and maybe I should let him. After all, he oversaw the assignments tonight. Andrea should have gone into that bathroom with Valentina. She shouldn't have been alone for one second.

I'm close to erupting and shooting every motherfucking person in this room, save her. Kai takes another step forward, further trying to shield the others. "Boss…"

"Explain. Why the fuck was she alone in that bathroom? I know damn well it's not against your delicate sensibilities to be in the ladies' room… you've fucked enough women in there that no one bothers calling you out when you enter. So explain why my wife was almost killed…because I'd really like to fucking hear it."

A soft whooshing sound is pounding in my ears. Like my heartbeat but cranked to max volume. He's speaking, but I can't even hear him. I grab the closest object and throw it against the wall. It shatters, and I can't even tell what it was. The destruction doesn't help.

I'm so angry I'm dizzy with it. All this time of caring for her, keeping her safe, helping her recover was shattered in a moment of carelessness. And worse, I blame myself too. I shouldn't have left her alone for one second. It should have been me in that bathroom with Valentina. Sal wouldn't have dared to show his fucking face.

I go to the bar, fling glasses out of the way until I find the bottle I want. It feels so breakable in my hands, yet I don't fling it away. I tug the cork out of the top and take a long draw, then turn to face Kai again. "I didn't hear a fucking word you said because there is no excuse you can give me that will make this fucking right."

I gesture at Valentina and then look at her. My words die in my throat. She's huddled in my coat, wide, glassy eyes staring at me in alarm. Now she's scared of me. Hell, she wasn't even scared of me when we met. She wasn't scared of me when she came to me for help. Sal did this, and I'll fucking slaughter him for it.

Ignoring my men, I slowly approach her. When she flinches away, it's like a knife in my gut, serrated and dull. "Angel, look at me."

She continues to stare straight again. I snap my fingers in front of her face and pat her cheek. "Val, darling, look at me."

When she shifts her gaze to mine, her face crumples, and the glossy sheen of her eyes morphs to tear-coated. "It's not their fault. I needed time alone. I told them to leave me alone."

"Why?" I plead for her to explain, to give me a reason not to kill my friends.

"Rose," she whispers. "I kept seeing her in the crowd. The night I met you, it was our first party, and we were so excited. I kept seeing her..." Her voice drifts off, and the tears stop falling.

I cup her cheek and turn enough to take the bottle and press it to her lips. "Take a little sip for me, Angel. You're in shock, and I need you to take a sip and let it help calm you down."

She blinks lazily and then does as I ask. Once she swallows, she looks at me again. "Adrian? What's going on? Please. Take me upstairs. I need..."

I'm already moving before she finishes her sentence. With the bottle still in my hand, I pick her up and carry her to our room, slamming the door behind me. She jolts at the sound but settles as I carefully set her on the bed.

I gently peel off the jacket and then ease off the dress hanging off her waist. She doesn't assist or try to stop me. Next, I ease all the pins from her hair and massage her scalp. Once I tossed them on her sink in the bathroom, I bring out a makeup remover wipe, and as thoroughly as possible, I wipe away her smeared makeup.

"Tell me what you need, Angel. I'm right here."

She reached out to cup my cheeks. "You. I just need you."

I move to get on the bed, but she stops me, scratching at the buttons of my shirt. After I start to quickly undress, she lies down on the pillows watching me. There's no heat in her gaze, no response to either of our nudity as I climb into bed naked beside her.

She curls up, her back to my front, and I pull her into me. "Angel?"

"Mm-hmm?"

"Talk to me. Are you okay?"

"Fine. I just need you to touch me. Chase away the memories and make them good again." As she speaks, she guides my hand down her belly to her pussy, urging my hand between her thighs.

"Did he touch you...?"

"No, he didn't get the chance. Rose..." She breaks off, and I wait, holding my breath.

When she doesn't continue, I prompt her. "Rose, what?"

"It's nothing," she murmurs and rolls over to face me. She rearranges my hand so I'm cupping her gently.

I want nothing more than to part her warmth and sink my fingers inside her. To give her something to chase away the pain, to erase that bastard from her mind, but I can't bring myself to touch her right now. Not because I don't want to, but because I don't trust myself to stop. Everything in me is screaming to claim her, mark her, take her as mine. But I can't do it with this glassy look in her eyes. Not when she still thinks I plan to give her up one day.

"Angel, talk to me. Tell me how to help you."

She wiggles against my hand and closes her eyes. "Touch me, please. I need you."

Fucking hell. There's only so much control a man can have. But she looks so fragile and so young spread out on my bed.

"I can't do that right now, Angel. Not until you're more like yourself."

Her lip quivers. "Then you don't want me. It was all a game. That's why we haven't had sex yet."

I roll her onto her back in one quick move, shoving between her thighs in the next. My hard cock is right against her, and I know she can't mistake it.

"Let's get one thing straight. I want you more than I want my next breath. I want to shove into your tight little body until you scream my name. And when I spill my load, I'll stay inside you until I know my child is growing in your womb. You're mine, and only mine, Valentina. I won't be letting you go anywhere."

Her eyes are wide now but calmer and more alert. A pink flush stains her cheeks, and I drop my mouth there, kissing her warm skin. "I'm trying to be gentle, Angel, but it's not in my nature. I only know how to take, and right now, it's all I want to do."

"Touch me, please," she whispers. Her hands cup my cheeks, and I stare down into her eyes. "Touch me and let me feel something other than fear, or anger, or pain. Give me pleasure to chase away this black hole inside me. It's threatening to eat me alive, and I'm so tempted to let it."

I press down on her so I can frame one of her hands, my other arm supporting some of my weight. "Don't you dare. You belong to me. We made a deal, remember? We haven't fulfilled any part of it yet."

She nods, her eyes wary. "I know. I thought maybe that's why…"

A hot wave of anger rolls over me. "If you're implying I let Sal get to you. That I would put you in danger as what…some kind of punishment for not being ready to have sex with me, then you better keep your fucking mouth shut. I would rather rip off my own arm than put you in danger."

She swallows loud enough for me to be able to hear it. "It's ridiculous. I know, I'm sorry. I didn't mean…"

I grab her chin and force her eyes to mine. "Is this you trying to fulfill our deal to ensure what happened tonight never happens again? Is that the only reason you're begging me to touch you? Some kind of payment?"

And just like that, the knife in my gut is back. Except this time, she's twisting it with her own bloodstained hands.

Fuck. I shove off her before I vent my rage on her fragile body. Instead of shouting, I pace around the room, trying to give myself time to process. If all of this is a lie to her, then where does that leave me? I never once pretended she wasn't my end goal. I'm not sure how long I pace. I only stop when a soft hand on my shoulder stills me.

When I turn to face her, tears are streaming down her cheeks again. Fucking hell, I hate when she cries. It tears things inside me I didn't even know I could feel anymore.

"I'm sorry. I'm so sorry. You've been nothing but kind and gentle with me. I shouldn't even have hinted you would let me get hurt. Your men aren't to blame either because I asked them to give me a minute. They were trying to be polite."

I turn away, intending to pace some more. Maybe walk back and forth across the hardwood until some of this rage burns out of me.

"Please, come back to bed."

I shrug her hand off me. "Why? What's the fucking point if I'm just some monster hell-bent on using you for your body in exchange for your protection?"

She clutches at me again and then turns me to face her. "Come back to bed, please. I want you to make love to me."

## 26

## VALENTINA

Saying it doesn't lessen my fear. He tips my chin up as if he can see right through me to the marrow. One look and I'm spread wide for his inspection, and somehow, he doesn't shy away from what he sees.

"How about a shower first, Angel? You're shaking."

I stare down at my hands, gripping his arm tightly, and my fingers are trembling. Strange that I didn't notice. Well, now I do, and the fact that my knees are knocking together.

Now that a shower is on the table, I realize how much I want one. Hot and steamy to get every trace of Sal off my skin. Scrubbed and clean like he never touched me at all. If only it were that easy. If only the years of enduring his touch weren't branded on my body.

He picks me up easily, slinging me into his arms. I wrap my hands around his neck automatically. Not because I fear he'll drop me but because I want to bury my face against him and draw that clean, masculine scent into my lungs.

He starts the shower with one hand and gently eases me onto my feet under the warm spray. It's hot and takes me a moment to adjust. Before

I can start on my hair, he spins me, his front to mine, and he backs me under the direct spray and goes to work on my hair himself. How can a man with such a ruthless reputation be so gentle to me? I lean my head into him so he can reach the back of my hair. Once he finishes washing, he adds conditioner and teases a comb through my curls like I showed him before. It melts my heart, and tears mix with the water as he silently works.

After the hair, he rubs a soap bar through his palms and then uses his bare hands to wash my body. He takes his time, easing his fingers over every inch of me and saving my pussy for last. Meeting my eyes, he sets his mouth in a firm line, then he slides his slick fingers between my legs and massages the soap everywhere. When his fingers graze my clit, I don't bother biting back the moan that rises in me. But he doesn't continue there, only kneels in the shower and washes my thighs, my calves, and my feet. He props one of my feet onto his thigh and gently eases the ache caused by the high heels I wore.

"Feel better?" he asks, still kneeling.

I delve my fingers into his wet hair, mussing it. "Let me wash you now."

He casts his eyes up the line of my body but then stands and lets me wash him. He must bend way down for me to reach his hair, and then I also take my time washing him carefully with the soap. His shoulders are impossibly wide, and they make a beautiful sight as you move from their width to the tightly muscled curve of his waist.

Damn, he's beautiful.

In suits, he's devastating, but like this...he is nothing but destruction. I can't stop touching him, even if I wanted to.

"Angel," he whispers.

I look up from where I'd been running my fingers along the indents at his hips. "Hmm...?"

"I don't think I have it in me to be gentle tonight. But I know that's what you need."

His hands are shaking as he wraps both of mine around the hard tip of his cock. It juts up between us, solid and hot.

"Help me, so I can be gentle with you afterward."

I notch my chin higher. "What if I don't want you to be gentle?"

He curses under his breath and backs me straight into the shower wall. His tall hard body presses tight into me. "I'm not playing games. When I say you can't handle it tonight, then trust me." He nips my bottom lip with his teeth hard enough to sting. "There will be other nights to exercise my control, but tonight isn't one of them. Nod, Angel, so I know you understand."

I nod, my breathing sounding loud to me, even with the spray of the water bouncing off the tiles around us.

He eases his feet back enough to give me room to work him while his upper body and face stay aligned with mine. It can't be a comfortable position, but I don't say anything and do as he asks.

I trust him.

Watching his face for his reactions, I move my hands up and down his length. I remember helping him do this before, but it seems more difficult on my own. He stands above me, watching my eyes, my lips, and then back up again.

I tighten my grip until he hisses out a breath, and then I work him faster. When his hips twitch forward in time with my movements, like he's thrusting into them, a hot molten core opens inside me. I'm burning from the inside out, and he's the only one who can quench the flame.

"Finish it, Angel," he grits out. "Harder."

I again follow his direction and pump him harder, faster, always watching his eyes. At first, he didn't appear to be reacting at all. But now, staring into his eyes, I see it. Not just the sensation of my hands on his body, but how much he wants me. How much he can't wait to make me scream his name. How hard he's going to take me despite his desire to go slowly with me.

I don't care. I want him more than anything right now. My strokes are shallowing out as my arms grow tired. He wraps his hands around me again and offers his own strength to mine. Together, we slick up his length and pump him faster. He's pressing more into me now, almost pumping himself against my belly.

And then a warm jet of cum hits my skin first, right under my breast. Then over a nipple. On my lip.

He never, not for one second, takes his eyes off me. When he eases himself down and carefully unpeels my fingers from his now semi-hard length, I realize my heart is hammering in my chest so hard I can hear it in my ears and feel it in my entire body. I'm throbbing with need for him.

He reaches out and swipes the drop of his semen off my lips, then gently shoves it into my mouth so I can lick it off. I wrap my tongue around his finger, lapping it all and then sucking deep so he knows what else I want to do to him.

"Still testing my control, I see. Let's go to bed so I can take care of you."

He flips off the water, steps out of the shower, and grabs a fluffy white towel. When I move to take it, he smacks my hand gently and then uses it himself to dry me from head to toe. Afterward, he grabs the product I use in my hair. I'm about to protest, but he gives me a look that freezes my bones where I stand. Message received. He wants to take care of me in every way. Not just the sex parts.

After he finishes and dries my hair again, he scoops me into his arms and carries me to the bed. He'd given himself a brisk wipe with the towel, and water droplets still cling to his skin in places. When he climbs onto the bed beside me, I turn and lick one off the curve of his shoulder.

I'm on my back with him between my thighs in the next second.

"Are you wet for me?" He delves his fingers through my pussy, testing me for himself. Then he licks his finger and settles his weight against my hips once more. "You are wet for me. Does jerking my cock turn you on?"

I swallow and nod hesitantly. Does he really want to know this? Or is he playing some kind of game with me? My inexperience hits me all over, and suddenly, I don't know what I'm doing. He leans in and nips my lower lip with his teeth to catch my attention. But he already has it. I can't take my eyes off him when he's like this. Like he lives and breathes just for me. No one has ever looked at me like this.

"I'm not done with you, Angel. Let me see how long it takes my sweet little Angel to scream for me." He dips his fingers inside me, then brings them up to catch my clit.

I'm shaking, and I don't know why. My heart feels like it might burst from my chest *Alien*-style at any moment. A laugh bursts from me, and I slap my hand over my mouth, eyes wide, as his narrow.

He freezes. "Are you laughing?"

I shake my head quickly, a hot flush clawing its way up my neck. "No. I'm so sorry. I didn—"

He tugs my hand off my face and takes my lips one more time. While he coaxes my mouth open, he rubs his cock against my clit, right where his fingers used to be.

When I lean up and into him, he pulls away. "You aren't laughing at this."

Then he angles himself again, this time, barely catching my entrance with the head of him.

I suck in a breath, holding it. Waiting...yearning...even as fear spikes through me.

"Relax, take a breath," he orders. This time, he notches himself right there, right where I want him and where I'm terrified he'll go.

But I shouldn't be, right? The second we do this, our deal is fulfilled, and I don't have to worry about anything. He'll take care of Sal, of me, of everything. In my mind, it sounds like the dream I had months ago with Rose. Freedom. While I may not be free...I don't think I want to be. I learned a long time ago there are way worse things to be scared of than being owned by a man who wants to take care of your every need. I know he's not perfect, hell, probably not even a good person, but who is in this world.

"Breathe, Angel. It'll only hurt for a second." He pushes into me slowly, taking his time as my body adjusts to his. He's with me every second, his forehead pressed to mine, even if the position forces him to arch his back to maintain it.

He watches me, and while I want to squeeze my eyes closed, it feels like abandoning him. So I keep my eyes on his as he finishes pushing into me. Everything feels tight and tingly. A flash of pain was in there somewhere, but pain doesn't mean the same thing to me as it does to others. I barely noticed it while staring at him.

"You're mine," he whispers. His jaw sets tight, and he pulls out and pushes back inside me. "You belong to me."

I nod because I can't get my voice to work. He stops moving, and everything in me is starting to tighten more.

"No, Angel. It's not enough. Say it. Say it for me, and I'll give you everything you want. I'll make you feel good."

My exhale comes out in a rush. "I'm yours," I whisper.

Instead of pushing into me again, he twists to the side, aligning us and entwining our legs. He pulls mine up onto his hip and guides us together. "Yes, you belong to me."

I arch into him. The pain is gone, and I can't feel anything but him. In my body, in my head, in my heart. I clutch at his shoulders, wanting him to give me more.

"I've got you, Angel." He presses into me again, not so much an in and out motion as just rocking, and it puts the top of his cock right at the sensitive bud of my clit.

God, how can this feel so good? I'm shaking from head to toe and grip him harder. My orgasm slams into me so hard I see stars on a landscape of black. His mouth hits mine while I'm still trying to recover, his lips devouring me, his tongue taking over. I give it back to him, all the pleasure he's giving me, trying to at least...

I feel him come hard, his breathing as erratic and shallow as mine. When he stops, everything is hot and sticky between us. He moves our legs around so he can stare down between us. There's a white splotch of his cum on my thigh that he scoops up with his fingers and presses back inside me.

"This stays inside you."

"We...didn't use a condom," I manage, realizing only now the possible consequences.

He nuzzles my neck, arching my hips into his to press us together. "And we won't. Every time I come inside you is a chance to get you pregnant with my heir."

I'm frozen against him. While we got married, I hadn't considered he was serious about it. That a baby might be something he wanted with me. But I can't.

No. Not while Sal is out there and can hurt my baby and me. Not when he always takes every bit of joy I have.

## 27

## ADRIAN

*I*n the morning, I stare down at her, so beautiful and serene spread across the white sheets. It felt good to finally take her and make her mine. Even if I saw doubts swimming in her eyes before she fell asleep in my arms. It'll take time for her to fully trust me but getting rid of her fiancé will go a long way to help that.

I slip out of bed, careful not to wake her, and dress quickly. There's something I need to do. If she hadn't needed me, then I would have done it last night, but I couldn't resist the plea in her eyes when she asked for me—me.

She is still passed out when I exit the bedroom and head toward the command room. As expected, when I enter, no one is there except Kai.

He's sitting at the table with his back to me, jacketless, wearing the same clothing he wore to the party last night. When I enter the room fully, he stands, his face lined with regret and self-recrimination. He knows what needs to be done too.

He doesn't get a warning. I hit him in the side of the face full force and send him back into the chair so hard it tips over, taking him down on top of it. A dull ache starts in my hand and then shoots into my wrist, but it doesn't matter. Justice must be paid, and he knows what he almost cost me.

I punch him again, and he still doesn't defend himself. But I can't quite reach him partially under the table, lying haphazardly over the chair, so I motion at him to stand again. He follows my order without a second thought, even knowing what comes next.

I flex my hand as I question him. "Did you find Sal?"

He leans his head back to keep blood from running down his face. "No, sir. He was gone. The others are still out searching for him."

"Then you've done nothing to redeem yourself. Are you ready?"

Completely resigned, he drops his hand and stares me down. Then nods.

I let the anger I felt last night course through me—the rage, the pain, but most of all, the terror. This time when my fist makes contact, he remains standing. His head merely snaps backward from the force of the hit. Pain has reached my shoulder, but it's nothing. Nothing. Nothing at all compared to what she endured last night as her attacker lay on top of her. As she fought for her life from the one man I told her I could protect her from.

I grab his shirt front in my fist and move to strike him again, but something clamps onto my hand. I barely have enough presence of mind to freeze and look.

Valentina is standing there, her eyes rimmed with tears. "Stop, please," she sobs. "He doesn't deserve this."

I shove at him and step back. "You're right." Then I take the gun off the table he loaded himself and press it to the center of his forehead. "He almost let you get raped or killed. He deserves more than a few bruises and a busted nose."

She reaches for the barrel of the gun, and I swing it away so she can't grab it. "Step back, Valentina, before you get hurt."

"No. This happened to me. It should be my choice."

Her words reach me, and I stare down at her. The white robe she's wearing is three sizes too big and sweeps the floor with each agitated movement. Her hair is curly and frames her face in a halo of gold-tinged brown. I lower the gun and focus on containing my rage long enough to end this.

"You're right, Angel. This is your retribution."

I grip her wrist and press the gun into her hand. It looks ridiculously oversized in her small palm. She moves like she wants to drop it, but I cup her fingers around the pistol grip and turn her to stand in front of me. With my body behind hers, I align our arms and cup her other hand to the other side. In this position, I can help her.

"Protecting you was his job. He failed. He understands what that means for him."

Tears are pouring down her cheeks now, and each one is like an ice pick to my gut. I hate to see her cry. Yet punishment must be dealt out. "He made a mistake. He doesn't deserve to die for it."

I lean down to speak into her ear. "And what if Sal had raped you? Would you be so lenient on him then? What if the last thing you saw was his greasy mug above yours? What if your last moments were spent in humiliation and pain?"

"S-Stop…" she sobs. "Stop it. Don't do this."

I grip her hands tighter, forcing them to the trigger. She's shaking against me and crying, and I can't take it. With a little shove away from her, I release my hold.

She stumbles forward, still holding the gun. Then as if realizing it, she flings out, trying to dislodge it. Kai gets to her first, catching the weapon, and deposits it safely on the table.

I turn to face her, grabbing her shoulders so she can look at me. "This is part of our world. If I can't trust him to keep you safe, then I can't trust him to do anything."

She sniffles hard, her cheeks red now. "But he's your friend."

"My friend wouldn't have let my wife be attacked." I glare over her shoulder as I say it. "My friend would have caught the bastard and presented him to me wrapped in a bow ready for me to take my vengeance on him."

"This is my choice, right?" she asks, her voice stronger now, her tears gone, only the dampness on her cheeks remaining.

When I don't answer, she cups my cheeks and guides my eyes to hers. "It's my choice? Since I was the one who was attacked, it should be. And I don't want him to die."

Fucking hell, I can deny her nothing. Not when she looks at me with those soft eyes and halo of curls for good measure. I stare at the gun and then at her. "His life is yours then to do with what you will. Kai is no longer my second but yours. But if he gets you killed, I swear to you, every single person involved will die."

She nods once and turns to face Kai, who wears a stunned expression, his face bleached of color. "She can't...what...?"

He cups the back of the chair with both hands and leans in like he needs the extra support. And maybe he does. It hurts to lose the one man I thought would get me through anything. The one man I could count on above all others. But, by the same token, I know if something else happens to her, he'll die to prevent it. His code of honor would allow nothing less.

"Any news on his whereabouts?" I demand.

He stares back and forth between Valentina and me, now unsure of who he should address. "No, nothing yet. But we did get a message from her father."

She gasps, and I pull her against me, wrapping my arms around her shoulders. "My father? How does...? Oh, someone from the party would have told him they saw me."

"That was the point. He would have learned of our marriage eventually," I tell her. Then to him. "Send word it's not going to happen, and get the others back here so we can discuss strategy."

He nods and fishes his phone out. The skin on his face is already swelling from hitting him, and my knuckles are a jagged mess. I'm still angry enough to beat him to death on my command room floor. The only thing standing between me and his death is five feet of too much fucking compassion.

She scans us both and rushes out of the room. When she's gone, I take a step toward him. "If something like this happens again, I don't care what I told her, I will put a knife to your throat myself. Are we clear?"

He rubs at his bloody nose with his shirtsleeve. "We're clear. It won't. I'll protect her with my life."

I shove at him. "You should have done that last night."

"Hey!" she shouts. "You said he's mine, and I don't want him hurt anymore."

She crosses between us and presses a plastic bag of ice to his cheek. The sight of her touching him makes me want to rip his arms off and beat the shit out of him with them. It's stupidly irrational, but I can't help myself. The only person who should touch her is me.

"Don't fucking touch him," I grit out, forcing everything in me to focus on something else. She enters my field of vision and takes my hand in her own, then presses another ice pack to my skinned knuckles. "I won't touch him again. I didn't mean to upset you."

I grab her around the throat, only hard enough so that she understands how serious I am. "If you touch another man, any man at all, I will kill him."

She gives me a shaky nod, and I can feel her gulp under my palm. When I release her, she clucks over my knuckles, and Kai starts to leave.

I grab him by the arm before he can go. When she starts to interfere, I glare down at her, warning her off. "The other thing I asked you to take care of?"

He points at a box on the table I hadn't even noticed. I let him slip out the door and grab the box.

She's curious and peers around my shoulder. "What is it?"

I tug her to my front and lift her easily to sit on the edge of the glass table. "A gift for you."

The light that enters her eyes at such a small statement clears the rest of the anger still seething inside me. Gods, no one could be angry at that look, nor the soft, warm feeling she puts inside me just with a look.

I open the box and pull out a cell phone, then turn it to face her. "It's for you. All our numbers are programmed inside. This way, you can call for help if you need it or order stuff online. Whatever you need."

"You...this is for me?" She blinks down at it, almost shocked.

I tuck a thatch of stray hair behind her ear, but of course, it doesn't stay. "It's just a phone, Angel. You're not a prisoner here. You belong to me, yes, and right now, I don't want you to go anywhere until we take care of Sal, but I still want you to live your life."

Tears coat her lashes again, and I brush them away. "Don't cry, please."

"It's just. I don't want to know what to do. I mean...my whole life was spent inside that house as a punching bag for my father, then worse when Sal showed up. My only plans were the ones he made and the ones I made to try to free us. Now, I'm not sure what to do with myself. I mean, I can't just stay here and live in your bed."

"Our bed," I correct her. "And if that's what you want to do, especially when you get nice and round with our baby, then that's what you'll do."

Her eyes go wide again, the same panicked look she gave me last night. She might not be keen on the idea of having a child now, but soon, she'll be pregnant with my baby. I can't wait to spoil them both and give them everything I didn't get as a child.

"Can we...talk about something else?"

I nudge her thighs apart and step between them to remove the tie of her robe. "Like what?" I ask, then bend down to nuzzle the curve of her neck. She squirms against me, and I love the breathy sigh that follows.

She threads her fingers into my hair and leans back on the table. "On second thought, maybe we should talk after."

## 28

## VALENTINA

It's been one month since we first had sex. In the real world, it's probably not a milestone people celebrate. But to me, giving my body in that way, feeling safe in it, comfortable with it, feels like something to celebrate.

When I wake and find the bed empty, I know he's already working, so I get dressed and hatch my plan. It starts by texting Kai. He arrives a few minutes later but refuses to enter my bedroom, so I drag him down the hallway to the room I started turning into a library.

Once inside, I close the door, and he looks ready to bolt. How can a grown man who worked as my husband's right hand for years be so skittish when I get him alone? I know Adrian can be jealous, but I'd never touch him. They both know that by now.

He inches toward the door as I study my progress in the room. "I need your help with something. I want to make Adrian a special meal tonight to celebrate. Do you happen to know anything about his mother?"

While turning the door handle, he freezes.

I stare at him, hands on my hips, and wait for him to face me, confusion all over his face. "Why do you ask about his mother?"

"He doesn't talk about her much, but I know they had a special relationship. Do you know if she ever cooked him anything special? Something that might bring back happy memories."

"I'm sure he will enjoy anything you make for him."

I'm missing something in his tone, I can tell. It's too light, too breezy as if he doesn't want me asking questions. But does he want me to stop questioning him or ensure I don't ask Adrian these things?

"Why are you so spooked? It's a simple request. I can go ask someone else if you don't know."

He blocks the door with his big frame. "No. That won't be necessary. Just give me a second to think about it."

I give him my sweetest smile. "Great. You have no idea how much I appreciate this."

Damn. The men around here are jumpy. As if I would ask Adrian about his mother directly, knowing how much talking about her hurts him. Andrea is a little easier to deal with, but she's often out on jobs with the team, so I don't see her as often as Kai. Who I think resents his new job. Not sure what he expected? Running my errands with me and lifting boxes might not be as exciting as whatever Adrian had him doing, but the other option was death, so in my mind, I think he should be a tad more grateful. Or maybe just a tad less squirrelly about me asking simple questions.

It takes a few minutes, but Kai finally answers. "He mentioned this soup his mother made him as a child when he was sick… I can't pronounce the word or even write it down, too many sounds, but when he explained it, he told me it was a traditional Czech garlic soup. Something they make for illness or hangovers."

I narrow my eyes and stalk toward him. "You're not just making this up, right? To get me to stop asking questions because I won't do that to him."

"No, I'm serious. We talked about it when we were recovering from a party in the pool."

It doesn't sound very romantic, though. Wait—I gape at him. "Pool?"

He points at the ceiling. "It's on the roof."

Excitement bursts through me. I love to swim. "Can we go up there?"

"Don't you have a romantic soup to prepare?"

He's right, but now that I know the pool is there, I won't forget. "Okay, I'll talk to the cook and get the stuff I need. You can go glower at something or whatever."

His mouth turns down hard. "I don't glower."

I stare at his lips, which some might consider pretty, and then let my gaze run back to his eyes again. Yeah...right. All the men in this house are professional brooders.

Thankfully, he slips out of the room with no further insight. I fish my phone out of my pocket and text the cook my shopping list. As usual, when I request something, she complains for about five minutes and then does as I ask. If only because she fears I'll tell Adrian she ignored my directives.

When I tell her she has to clear the kitchen for the night, she's going to be pissed, but it'll be worth it once I present my gift to Adrian. I just want him to know what this time of safety, this freedom, has meant to me.

I putter around the library until someone interrupts with lunch. There's too much to do, but I want to get things ready for dinner. First, I send Adrian a text asking him to meet me for dinner at seven in the kitchen. He agrees but immediately asks why.

I can't help but smile when I send him back a kissy face emoji and nothing else. But I better get to the kitchen before he tries to find me to get answers.

The kitchen is deserted when I enter, and my grocery requests are lined up neatly on the counter. Cook is efficient, I'll give her that. She hates me, but I still intend to win her over one of these days.

According to the recipe I found, the soup isn't much more than a garlicky potato soup. It looks good, and the recipe says it's the traditional soup for illness. Either way, I suspect Kai is right, and he'll love it all the same. But just once, I want to feel like I accomplished something. It might be small, but I've latched onto the idea, the fantasy of seeing the joy written on his face, and I can't let it go.

Once the soup is done, I have to admit it smells delicious. I set out the bread, wine, and salad to go with it. It takes me a few minutes to change into a white lace dress I know he loves and make it back to the kitchen before he saunters in.

But when he does, damn. He seems to take up the entire room. His posture is carefree and effortless, but I can spot the power in his wide shoulders, the muscles in his long legs. He's a cobra ready to strike, and tonight, I'm his prey.

"Thanks for coming," I say meekly, undone by the dark need in his eyes.

He takes the seat I pulled out for him, and I sit beside him on the other. "What did you do, Angel?"

I ladle some soup into the bowl and serve the bread, wine, and salad next. When I finish, I turn to face him, studying his features for any clue to his response.

"Angel..." he whispers. When he looks up at me, the need has changed to something softer, gentler. "You made this for me?"

"I asked Kai. He told me you mentioned it before, and I wanted to do something special for you. To make you feel cared for, for once." I tuck my chin and face my own food so he can't see the blush on my cheeks at my own admission. Things between us are different for him, different from what I want between us. I don't blame him, not one bit, but I still want him to know how much I appreciate the effort he's gone through to maintain our agreement. Not that spending night after night underneath him, screaming out in pleasure is much of a hardship for my side of things.

He leans down and takes a tentative bite. I'm on the edge of my seat with nerves. I've cooked a little bit in my life but not much because I've always had chefs. But cooking for someone seems like something a caring person would do. A way to feed them and show them they are loved and wanted.

"It's delicious. Thank you," he whispers a few seconds later.

I hide my face again so he can't see what his praise does to me. How it makes me squirm, not only in happiness but in a different way.

When we finish eating, he turns to me and pulls me onto his lap. It's an awkward position on the stool, but he seems to make it look effortless. "There's something I want to show you now. Will you come with me?"

I nod, shifting off his lap, but he lifts me into his arms as if I weigh nothing and trots off out of the kitchen and down the hall. When I wrap my arms around his neck, he resettles me and takes me up a few flights of stairs. The distance is easy for his long legs as he takes two risers at a time.

When we get to the top, he nudges the door open with his hip, and we step out into the darkness. Well, it's mostly dark. As we come around a corner, I gasp. There's the pool Kai mentioned, and above it, the stunning city skyline on display.

I wiggle for him to release me and race to the edge of the clear glass railing. "It's so beautiful." I have to shout through the sharp wind ripping around us.

"Come here," he whispers in my ear, tugging me back into him. I go with zero hesitation.

With his arms around me and the warmth at my back, I could stay like this for hours, watching the glittering lights of the city blink out one by one.

"I have something else for you, Angel."

I turn to look at him. "I don't need—"

He picks me up again, this time around my ass. I automatically lock my legs around his hips, spreading myself wide. It only takes a few strides for him to get to the wall by the stairwell. Then another second to shove my dress up, rip my panties at the seams, and drive inside my body with his.

I freeze against him, and he follows suit, giving me a moment to adjust to the sheer size of him. But the tension in his shoulders tells me he's not going to be easy with me, not this time. And I don't mind. I feel a little wild myself staring at the buildings like anyone could look out their window and see us fucking against the wall.

"Please," I say and dig my fingers into the back of his neck to pull slightly on his short hair.

He arches his hips into me and then sets a brutal pace. His hands around my ass, tugging me to meet him, protects my skin from the scratch of the wall after each brutal stroke.

There's nothing to do but cling to him and feel my body stretch around him, sparking pleasure along my nerve endings. I'm so wet I can feel it on my thighs, on his stomach, everywhere. I don't know where it came from, but I throw my head back, leaning it against the wall, and let him take me hard and fast.

"Please," I say again, then it's more like a plea, a mantra, a hymn as I repeat the word over and over. The wind snatches each syllable, but I know he hears me. He fucks me faster, deeper, almost painfully now, driving us both toward the end I need in my soul.

I dig my fingers into his scalp, my fingernails cutting deep. His pace falters once, and I know he's close. When I tug on his hair and scratch at the back of his neck with my other hand, he shoves into me once more, his cock brushing me just right that it sets off an orgasm so hard I can't even breathe through it. I'm shuddering, head to toe, and finally, I suck in a long drag of air, the sensation washing through me as he reaches his own end.

As usual, once he finishes, he stays inside me for a few moments, growing softer in my pussy until finally, he slips out. Then he sets me on my feet and gently eases any fluids that have escaped back into me.

"Let's go to bed, Angel. There is a lot more I have to say about this gift?"

I blink, suddenly nervous, as I tug my dress straight. "Like what?"

"Don't worry. I'll give you feedback while my mouth is between your pretty thighs and my lips are on that sweet cunt of yours."

He doesn't wait for me to answer, just lifts me into his arms and carries me to our bed.

## 29

## ADRIAN

Vincent, my third, isn't Kai. The hard part is I shouldn't be mad at him because he's not Kai. It doesn't keep me from throwing a little more effort into sparring with him in the gym before we start the day. He takes my latest hit with a grunt and then rebounds with a strike to my ribs that will hurt later. I appreciate him not pulling any punches because of who I am. It's something I've always liked about him.

We square off again and go a few more circles. The mats around us groan and squeak as our bare feet move across the surface. Across the room is exercise equipment the others use more than I do. I usually find the release I need right here, punching things until they tell me to stop.

Vincent gets in a jab on my shoulder, and I know I'm distracted. "Let's see you do that again, Kid."

He's one of the younger men on the team and doesn't appreciate me pointing it out. Instead of another strike, he sweeps his legs out but not fast enough. I dance away, careful to avoid another swipe if he's got any fancy ideas.

We continue until my arms are so tired it takes effort to hold them up. A sharp chime on my phone ends things for the morning completely. I check the message and then glance at Vincent, who is opening his texts too. Kai sent them to both of us.

I strip the gloves off my hands and grab a towel and a water on my way out the door to the command room.

Kai is there, looking impeccable as always. I deliver a glare as my greeting, but Vincent claps him on the back and throws his long frame into the seat next to him. "What's up?"

Kai grabs a couple of pieces of paper off the printer, handing one to each of us. I don't bother hiding my impatience. "Don't you have things to do that involve keeping my wife safe?"

Despite the set of his shoulders screaming out his anger, he doesn't show any of it on his face. A skill I always admired in him. "This does involve keeping her safe. Will you just read it? Please?"

Vincent lets out a low whistle and tosses the sheet on the table, then looks at me, waiting. Well fuck. This can't be good if he doesn't just give me the summary version in passing. Who prints out emails these days?

I cross one arm under the other and scan the sheet, slowly taking in the words, even as something dark and dangerous builds inside me as each new word collides with the next. When I finish, I crumple the email in a ball and launch it across the room.

"What the fuck is that old man playing at? He thinks he can snap his fingers, and the council will grant his wish to get her back?"

I wave at the sheet. "That's a load of shit, and he knows it. So what's the point? The second I produce our marriage certificate, they can't deny anything. She's not going back, so why put in the effort?"

"A trap?" Kai supplies. "The council will want to see you both, in person, to make sure she is well and not being coerced. It's a smart play at getting you both in one location at a specific time and place."

"I don't like it," Vincent chimes in.

I roll my eyes and pace across the room, back and forth from the door to the wall. The council will deny his petition. It's as simple as showing them the proof of what she looked like when we found her. There is video evidence, and the medical charts the doctor kept, then the marriage certificate. It's not so hard to believe that I saved her life, and she fell in love. They can't deny a love match any more than they do a marriage of alliance.

Doubts hit me, pummeling through the surety. I still haven't taken care of Sal. What if she changes her mind about being with me and then tells the council something that will let them take her away?

I stalk to the table and pound my fists onto the cold glass. Not hard enough to break the surface, but enough to make my knuckles and wrists sting from pain. "There is nothing they can do to take her from me, and if the council requests my presence, then we'll have to get creative on how to meet them, so no other interested attendees crash the party."

Kai takes a risk and speaks up again. "What I don't get is why make the effort? He never cared about her. We saw what she looked like when we got her out of that house...and he's never shown any kind of affection at parties or events. Hell, we'd only seen her at one, and before then, he never once mentioned her existence. Like he wanted to erase her from his life completely. Maybe Sal was his attempt at doing that, and it failed, so now he's trying to clean up the mess he made before he's implicated."

I stare down my former second. "You think her father knew where things would go with Sal and hoped he'd solve the problem of his daughter's existence for him?"

Kai shrugs. "Why not? He's not known to be the most ruthless of us for nothing. Just because things have been calm in his territory for some time doesn't mean he's stopped enforcing the law there. I think he's just gotten so good at it, he doesn't leave a trace of evidence behind."

I consider what he's saying, and it makes me sick. With this new idea, I have to turn away so they don't see how much I want to fucking rip out his guts. But it makes the most sense out of any other theories I've created on my own. Why else allow a man like Sal into Val's life? When there was evidence easily seen on her skin of how he treated her, yet the man never made a move to protect her.

"I have other news," Kai says, drawing me from the edges of a fugue that would likely result in bloodshed.

I turn. "What?" I grit out. "What else could have possibly gone wrong this morning?"

He looks almost apologetic when he answers. "Sal resurfaced but then disappeared again. His family is hiding him, for sure."

"That's better news than that fucking email. At least you have a location, right? We storm it and drag his fucking ass out."

Kai and Vincent wince, and I realize why. The season fucking ended over a month ago, or more...I haven't been keeping track with my focus on making Valentina comfortable in our bed.

If I make a move on them when the season is closed, it's an act of war against them and the council as a whole. One or the other, I might be able to deal with some damage, but not both, not at the same time, and not if the council calls the other families as allies to protect them.

Yet don't they deserve to be annihilated if they align themselves with Val's father against me? Isn't that the very definition of corrupt? Not considering other sides, only the ones who pay the most. Not that it mattered, but I could out-pay her father ten times over if I wanted to.

I think back to the night of the party and the few precious minutes which almost cost me so dearly. The few minutes I let her out of my sight when I'd met up with Nic Diavolo. Now, I wondered if his information stayed updated or if he would no longer be able to provide what I wanted.

I pace the room again, considering. Diavolo is a titan in his own territory, his own city, and he doesn't play games. If he knows where Sal is, he won't lie about it. But he'll also ask a steep price for the information. He is a businessman after all, and his second, Soo, is the same.

"We might have another option to find Sal and keep him this time." I stop and look between Kai and Vincent. "Diavolo."

"What about him?" Vincent asks, not having been there when I met with him that night.

Kai fills him in. "He might have Sal's exact location or know how to get it. He met with the boss the night of the season end party."

Realization dawns, and Vincent looks uncomfortable, realizing Diavolo was who I had been with when Val got attacked. No one wants to mention the incident, or anything related to it, for fear I might fly off the handle and pummel something. They aren't wrong. The closer I get to Val, the more frayed my patience has become, especially when the possibility of losing her is brought up.

I need to see her, touch her, reassure myself she is real, and here, and mine. Instead of making plans, I turn to the door and stop. No. I need to see her, but her safety always comes first.

With a groan, I turn back to them and grip a chair to calm myself. "Set up a meeting with Diavolo. Somewhere discreet where we can sit and have a meal, really chat. I'll see if I can get him to open up about what he knows or find out more about his connections to Sal's family. It's unlikely, but I'll try. He'll also have a few people with him, so make sure we have enough place settings. Cook can coordinate the meal and cook on-site. She won't mind the extra pay for the additional meal prep that day."

I take a moment to meet both their eyes. "Most importantly, Val doesn't know a thing about any of this. Do you understand? I'll tell her I'm going to a business meeting, and she will be content with that. I don't want her worrying while I'm gone, especially if nothing comes of it."

They both nod in agreement, and I stare at the currently blank screen on the wall. Just my fuzzy reflection stares back. "Maybe bring in a couple of girls we know. They can flirt and loosen things up."

I haven't thought of a single other woman since I met Val, and I don't plan to start, but that doesn't mean some of the single men will pass up the opportunity. "Make sure they are paid well and know they can leave at any time. But anyone who sticks it out will get more."

"Anything else, boss?" Kai asks.

I glare at him and look at Vincent. "Make sure everything is perfect. Kai can run back up to you if you need any additional help. Andrea too. She's good at these sorts of things."

"I had another idea in mind," Kai says, knowing he is playing with the nitrogen vapors of my patience right now. Fucking ballsy bastard.

He continues without prompting because if I speak to him one more time, I might deck him. As much as I want to let things go, I can't stop seeing the jagged cut of her dress and the bruises on her skin, and my rage returns.

"I might have a guy in the old man's security. It's an angle I've been working at for a while, and it seems, with all the changes lately, payments have been slipping, and some of his staff is unhappy. After seeing what happened to Valentina, a large chunk of them are."

I grip the chair again, digging my nails into the leather to ground me. "They saw her like that, and they didn't do shit to help her? Stop it? Stop him from hurting her so brutally?"

Kai realizes he took a misstep in bringing it up. He tries to backtrack. "The security contact was with him in New York, so he was unaware of what was happening at the house."

I shake my head and walk out of the room. Not for one damn second do I believe the security at the house and the security with Val's father didn't stay in constant contact. They chose to look the other way, and for that, they'd all die when I finally wrap my hands around that old skeleton's neck and squeeze the life out of him.

# 30

## VALENTINA

*I* watch him get on the elevator to go to his business meeting, and it hurts to see him leave. Rationally, I know he is coming back, but I miss him, and I am trying to rectify that with everything that has happened to me recently.

When the numbers on the elevator reach the ground floor, I'm tempted to go to bed and wait. Instead, I head to the kitchen to grab something to eat. He plans to be gone through dinner, which means I'm on my own.

Maybe that's the hard part. I've never been on my own. I always had Rose by my side when I needed company. A wave of grief hits me hard as I walk to the kitchen. Sometimes, I think I'm okay until I remember all over that she's gone. It weighs me down and makes it hard to think beyond it.

The only person in the room is the cook, who is bustling around prepping meals for tomorrow. Which I find strange since there aren't a ton of people in the penthouse regularly. Adrian's five are usually out doing whatever business they get assigned. Maybe she just likes to stay busy.

I plop on a stool, lay my hands on the countertop, and rest my face against them. "Did you make anything for dinner? Or should I make something for myself?"

For such a short, round woman, she sure moves fast. I watch her flutter some more, and then she huffs loud enough I can hear her. But she always makes those noises around me, as if my existence taxes her. "Of course I made something, and I don't want you messing up my workspace."

I sit quietly and watch her work, content not to be alone for a little while. She sets a bowl of fresh ramen in front of me and then turns to start typing on her cell phone. I dive into my noodles while she works on cleaning more perfectly immaculate stainless steel.

I take a bite and groan. "This is delicious, thank you."

As usual, she gives me a grunt of acknowledgment and goes about her work again.

I scarf down the delicious noodles and head to the sink to wash up my dishes. She waves me away, and I sit at the counter again. "Are you sure I can't help?"

"You have no idea where anything goes, and I don't want to find something out of place when I try to look for it." Her tone is gruff, but I've gotten used to it, so I simply shake my head.

I don't point out that the only dishes I tried to wash were a bowl and a fork...two things I definitely know the whereabouts of in the kitchen.

"You still here?" she says a moment later after she dries the offending dishes and puts them away.

"Sorry, I'll leave you alone." A part of me wishes she would call me back, but as I leave, I know she won't. The woman is not big on small talk.

I head to the little room I've been turning into a library and stare at the partially full shelves. He's given me every single book here, paying for it all as if it means nothing. I should feel guilty, right? Not only did he save my life but he's also given me safety, comfort, luxury here. I've always lived with money, but I never felt like I could request things or spend it. My father barely sprang for new clothes when necessary, and usually only if I ever had to be seen in public where he could be humiliated if I didn't play the part of the pampered princess. If only the others saw the bruises underneath the cashmere and lace. Then again, knowing more about the society now, maybe not. It seems everyone has a hidden underbelly of malice. It's just rarely seen unless provoked.

I consider this as I shelve books and neatly line them up with the edges of each dark wood shelf. It's satisfying to see them all perfectly organized by height and color. And it makes me feel good to have this space for myself.

In some tiny part of my brain, I have to admit that I'm waiting for the other shoe to drop. To learn some deep dark secret of Adrian's past that I'm going to have to pay for. Or worse, for Sal to walk out of that elevator one day and finally end my life.

A knock on the door sends my heart into my throat, and I'm already heading toward it when it's pushed open. But I should have known it wasn't Adrian because he doesn't knock.

Kai is standing in the doorway. "Are you okay? Do you need anything?"

I narrow my eyes. "Did he send you in here to check on me? Or are you just as bored as I am when he's not here?"

"Just doing my job. He says to keep you safe, so I keep you safe. Even if it's protecting you from paper cuts."

I huff out a laugh and turn back to the shelf, my excitement fizzled. He'll be home soon, and then I can throw myself at him. It's not healthy to feel so attached. I know this, yet I don't want it any other way. Not while Sal is still out there.

"Can I ask you something?" Kai says, still hovering in the doorway.

I thought he'd walk out when I turned away. "Of course, what's up?"

"Have you thought your relationship out? With Adrian, I mean? You do realize once he deals with Sal that he is going to have to deal with your father as well? It's the only way he'll feel his father's murder is avenged."

I'd heard my father killed his, but I'd never heard that from him directly. Nor could I deny it was probably true.

The vision of a pool of blood reflecting moonlight hits me. A memory from when I was a little girl. No, my father is no stranger to killing, and he has no qualms about making exceptions for women and children. The only reason I'm still alive was my usefulness as a bargaining chip.

I study him. He gives the impression of being perfectly put together, but the more I get to know him, the more I see the cracks underneath. "Let me ask you something...why do you care? I understand you protect Adrian and his interests, but why does my presence seem to threaten you, or does it threaten him in some way? So you want to protect him?"

He gives absolutely nothing away on his face. Just wears the same ole charming mask he usually does. "You don't threaten me, Valentina. It's not you. It's whatever is happening between you and him. He's already compromising in places he never would have to keep you safe. He's pushing himself to his limits, and I can see the effect it's having on his hard-fought control. And no one likes what happens when he loses control."

Now I just assume he's trying to scare me. After everything Adrian has done for me, I don't think there's a single thing I wouldn't do or endure for him. "Are you trying to scare me, Kai? Because I've faced scarier situations than a lecture in a library."

We don't need to discuss it. I can see that he was there the night Adrian saved my life.

He taps the doorframe and gives me a nod. "I suppose you're right. I just want you to be prepared for the inevitable. Soon, his control will fracture. It might not be you, or me, or anyone here, but when it goes, he'll be elemental in his rage. I hope you have the good sense to get out of the way when it happens."

When he leaves, I stare at the door for a few more moments. It's not as if I'd been living under a delusion that Adrian is some hero—none of us are—but he makes me feel safe, and I can't imagine a situation in which he wouldn't. Even pushing at my limits, he refuses to hurt me.

I go back to my shelf until my phone chimes from the table I'd set it on. Again, my heart leaps into my throat, and my chest feels tight. Hell, even my fingers tingle as I open the text messages to see a new one. It's from a number that isn't saved in my phone, but he might have borrowed one of his guys' to send me a message.

I wait for the image to load, and then I click on it. But it's not from him. It's of him. And he's not alone in the image. I squint down at the screen and then flip it to make it larger. He's at a dinner table, food and plates litter the table, and he's leaning in to talk to a woman.

One I remember very well from a certain hotel bathroom. I slowly lower myself down onto the crate holding books and stare at the screen. Then I click away and find more images, these ones zoomed in. Adrian is leaning in to seemingly whisper in her ear or kiss her neck. She's smiling, and that smile cuts through me.

My hands shake, and tears blur the screen. I don't know if I'd be less angry if it had been someone besides her.

Another part of my brain says I don't have any claim on him. He's claimed me, sure, but only to keep his end of the bargain and make sure I'm safe. But I can't exactly demand he be mine, and only mine, not after everything he's given me.

All of the logic doesn't matter because all I want to do is wring her pretty long neck and drag her away from him by the hair. The visual is violent, and I'm a little shocked at myself. But not shocked enough to feel guilty about it. Not when he's touched every inch of my body with his lips. Not when I've done the same to him. Not when he's the only person alive I feel safe around. I can't lose that, even if it means dealing with him sleeping with his ex.

A wave of nausea hits me, and I double over, covering my mouth. Nope, can't puke on the books. I rush out of the room and make it to the bathroom in time to throw up my ramen dinner.

After I lever myself off the cold tile floor, I brush my teeth and wash my face with a cool washcloth.

I dumped my phone on the bed, and I rush back to it to check the images again. Maybe they are old, maybe from when they were together? I grasp onto this excuse and climb into bed. My stomach is roiling, and tears cloud my vision.

If putting up with him sleeping with someone else means I stay safe, then it's just what I have to do. It doesn't mean it won't tear my heart to pieces in the process.

## 31

## ADRIAN

When the meeting ends, all I want to do is grab my Angel and crawl into bed with her. Usually, when it comes to business, I don't feel anything, really. But tonight, my meeting with Nic Diavolo turned into a reunion. His contact for the information insisted on being present, and she and I have a history. I also owe her for whatever part she played in Sal's attack on Valentina. I don't think for one second she didn't assist or clear the way for Sal to get into that restroom.

At first, I had to play nice with her. It wouldn't have helped my alliance with Nic if I'd shot her in the head at the dinner table. Despite its arrangement by my cook, that might be too far for even him. But it didn't keep me from feeling for the gun in the holster at my side every so often. A promise to myself that I would seek justice soon enough.

Once she revealed Sal's location, I shook hands with Diavolo and left before I did something that would jeopardize my alliance with him. At least until I found out the purchase price for the loss of his contact. Then I'd set one of my five on her, and she'd never be found again.

Right now, as I ride the elevator to my penthouse, I only want to see her. A moment to reassure myself she is still here and safe. If she left, I don't know if I could handle it.

When the doors open, I immediately scan the foyer for her, but it's late, so of course she won't be here waiting for me. Biting back my disappointment, I check her library first. She likes to work late in there. I finally find her in the bedroom, where I should have checked first.

The lights are still on, and I stop in the doorway, looking her over. Her clothes are still on, and she's curled up on the covers facing away from the door.

I walk around the end of the bed to the other side. Her eyes are open, and I kneel to stare into them at her level. Her face is red like she's been crying, and my heart takes a tumble at the thought. Was she upset I left?

I rub my thumb across her cheek, but she jerks away. "What's wrong, Angel? I wasn't gone very long, and Kai was here. No one could have gotten to you."

She sniffles and scoots farther across the bed so I can't reach her. I narrow my eyes and stand. "Angel?"

"I'm fine. Really. It's nothing."

I hate her moving away from me, but I give her a moment to come to her senses. "What's the matter? Tell me."

Another sniffle and she shakes her head. "Nothing."

I slide into the bed and grasp her hips so she can't move farther. "Bullshit. You're cowering away from me right now."

A new light enters her eyes, and she sits up, jerking from my grasp. "I'm not cowering."

"Then what are you doing? Because it feels a hell of a lot like you're not letting me touch you right now."

She jumps off the other side of the bed and paces next to it. "How did your meeting go? Did you have fun?"

I'm baffled by the change of subject. "Fun? It was a business meeting? I would never call them fun. I thought you knew where I was going."

She spins toward me, charging forward, and I have to admit this fierce, fiery side of her is turning me on.

"I knew where you were going, but I didn't know who else would be there."

It's my turn to show my teeth. I stand and button my suit jacket, then saunter around the bed to stare her down. "I didn't think I needed to clear my business associates with you before I meet with them."

She can talk to me any way she wants if she's prepared to pay the consequences for it. And right now, I'm ready to deliver those consequences personally.

She continues to pace, then faces me again. "I saw you together. Things didn't look very businesslike to me."

"What the fuck are you talking about, Val? You better start clarifying before I decide I'm done listening to you talk and just bend you over the bed for your punishment for speaking to me this way."

The mere mention of punishment before sent her running. Now, she turns to the bedside table and picks up a glass. Brandishing it at me, she yells. "You were with that skank, and I am angry, okay?"

The glass shatters against the wall before I realize she threw it. An impressive throw and would be worth the little show if she didn't look completely shocked right now.

"First off, Valentina, you need to calm the fuck down. Asking a question might be a better way to get answers from me rather than you being pissy and throwing things."

Her hands are shaking at her sides, and she's staring at the indent in the wall where the glass had hit.

"Angel?" I prompt.

She blinks and stares up at me again. This time, the spark of her anger is doused in a fresh round of tears. Then she stares down at her trembling hands. "Who am I becoming? I don't do this. I don't throw things or scream at people."

I take a step toward her, and when she doesn't skitter away, I gather her into my arms. "Or maybe you've never felt safe enough to voice your true feelings. When something upset you, which I assume happened often in that house of yours, you tucked it away and let it fester. Some part of you knows you are safe with me, and it's making you bolder. I'm proud of you."

She snorts against my chest. "You say that now, a moment after you talk about punishing me for it."

I delve my fingers into her messy curls. "Oh but Angel, I'm going to have so much fun punishing you, and I promise, by the end, you'll be begging me for my cock."

Her laughter soothes some of the edges inside me. Things that turned sharp at her anger. I don't know if I'd prepared myself to bite back at her or her enemies. Either way, it's something to consider later.

I continue to massage her scalp. "Tell me what happened? You said you saw me? I know you didn't leave this penthouse, so how did you see me?"

When she pulls away, I almost want to drag her back, but I want answers right now more. "I got a text."

She retrieves her phone and brings it over to show me. The number isn't one I recognize, nor is it one programmed into her phone. I scan the images and see how she could think I was getting cozy with my ex. At the same time, it hurts. She's the only woman I've been able to see since the moment I laid my eyes on her. No one else compares to her, and she thinks I'd go off and spend time with my ex because I felt like it.

I close her phone and toss it on the bed. "First, I'm going to find out who sent those pictures and make them pay for causing you distress. Second, I have a knife with her name on it, and when those pictures were taken, I was telling her in minute detail how I want to carve her up for the pain she caused you. But what I really want to know is why you're so upset? How could you think I'd want anyone else but you?"

Now she refuses to meet my eyes, my demure Angel back in place. "I just...I mean...I know I don't have any claim on you or anything. It just upsets me to see you with her, is all. If that's what you want to do, then I understand."

I grab her chin and force her eyes to mine. "As I said, all I want to put inside her is a six-inch stiletto blade so I can watch the life leave her eyes."

She blinks at me a few times, saying nothing.

"Does that scare you?" I ask, stepping closer to close the distance she keeps putting between us.

When she licks her lips, I focus on the path her tongue takes over them. "No. It should, right? I should be terrified of you, but you're the only man who has ever taken care of me and stood up for me. I told myself if you needed to have your ex, that it was a price I'm willing to pay to remain safe."

I tighten my grip, but she doesn't flinch. "And what about the other way around? What do you think I'd do if I ever found another man touching you?"

"Umm..."

"Use your imagination, Angel, because I promise you, if anyone so much as looks at you, I will definitely use mine. No one better so much as breathe in your direction."

"Yes, but it's different for you. This is just a de—"

I cut her off with my mouth, slamming my lips into hers hard enough our teeth scrape together. When I lift my face again, she's dazed and heavy-lidded. "You keep saying this is some kind of deal, but it's not for me. I didn't need to marry you if that were the case. Let me tell you for the final time, you belong to me, and if anyone tries to take you away from me, they will pay with their life."

She shakes her head, some of the lust clearing from her eyes. "I don't want anyone to die because of me. Not again…"

"Again?"

This time, she squeezes her eyes shut and rushes forward into my arms. I hold her and wait for her to get her courage up.

"When I was a little girl, a woman died right in front of me. My father, as you can guess, killed her. I was the one who handed him the gun, but I was too young to understand what he was about to do with it. Most of the details are hazy, but I remember the road was wet, and there was a puddle of blood leaching into a puddle of rainwater, and the moon reflected off it so brightly. All I could do was focus on the moon's reflection until my father led me away. That woman died because of me. Rose died because of me. I can't be the cause of any more deaths, please."

I hug her tight and then lead her to sit on the bed. She still won't look at me, as if she's ashamed. "Angel, you were a child. No matter how you might have assisted in that woman's death, you weren't at fault. I don't care if you stood over her and pulled the trigger. Your father was responsible, and I find it reprehensible he'd let a child feel responsible for that her entire life."

She gives me a watery smile, and I continue, sharing only what Kai knows about me. "My father wasn't the same as yours. Just as ruthless, to be sure, but he did his own killing, and he forced me to watch every single one so I could one day become the head of our family. When I refused, he'd force me, tie me down and pry my eyelids open."

Her warm hands cupping my cheeks drag me out of the memories. "Oh, I'm so sorry you had to go through that. How old were you?"

I cage her hands under mine. "It was a long, long time ago. I think it started when I was four. But it's in the past, and my bastard father is dead. We don't need to worry about him anymore."

There's nothing more to say about him. Nothing I'm going to tell her, not with her history with her own father and my future with him.

I make a mental note to get one of my guys to research this dead woman. Any skeletons in her father's closet are skeletons I want to line up in a neat little row to shove his way when the time comes.

## 32

## VALENTINA

With sunlight shining in the room so brightly, I have to cover my face with my arm. It helps hide the heat in my cheeks as I remember how I acted last night. How I overreacted.

I risk a glance from under my elbow to stare at his bare back. He's usually up and working well before I get up, but whatever happened last night took the energy out of him. His shoulders are wide and muscular, and my fingers itch to trace a path across them from the top of one shoulder to the other. His skin is darker than mine but not so dark that it looks like he spends any time in the sun. Right below his right shoulder blade rests a tiny brown splatter-shaped birthmark. I wonder if he knows it's there or if anyone has bothered to tell him.

I lean in and press my lips to that spot, then freeze, realizing what I'm doing. It was one thing to touch him as part of our agreement, fulfilling my side of our deal, but it's entirely another to crave his fingers on my skin and to want to press my lips all over him.

He stirs under me, and I scoot back in case he rejects me. He's claimed my body in one way or another plenty of times, but I don't think I can stand if he actually pushed me away.

"What are you doing, Angel?" he asks, rolling in the bed to face me. Before he's even flat on his back, he's drawn me into the curve of his arm. He smells even more strongly of the spicy ginger scent I associate with him right now, and I press my face into his ribs and breathe him in.

"As much as I'd love to see what you'll do next, baby, I have a meeting with the five in a few minutes. While I can keep them waiting, we have important business to handle."

He pulls me in tight in almost a hug, then hops out of bed naked, heading toward the bathroom. My eyes burn with oncoming tears, and I stare at the partially open doorway.

What the hell? I don't even know why I'm crying right now. He didn't reject me. He just has work to do, and I can't expect him to stay in bed with me all day.

I swipe at the tears and lie back on the pillow, trying to get control of myself. I've never been a crier. At some point, you learn tears don't make anything better, so why am I all of a sudden a blubbering mess whenever I think about him being away from me?

I drag the covers over my head so he doesn't see me when he comes out of the bathroom. When the water shuts off, I huddle deeper into the soft bedding and listen for the sound of his bare feet on the floor as he walks to the closet.

"Why are you hiding, Angel? Don't make me climb under there and find out for myself." His voice is deep and edges with steel that cuts so sweetly. I close my eyes and fall into it, calming myself. Then I throw the covers off and stare up at him. He's naked, standing a few inches from the edge of the bed, his eyes locked on my bare skin.

I flush hot and look away, unable to keep my eyes on all of him. There's too much to look at, too much to want to touch. "I'm fine. It's nothing."

He crawls across the bed until his knees brush my hip, then he drags my chin to the side so I'm meeting his eyes. "Don't lie to me, Angel. When something is wrong, you better tell me, or I can't do anything to fix it."

Tears threaten to fall again. "What if you can't fix it?"

"I can fix anything, Angel, even death." His voice gentles. "Tell me why you're crying."

I slap my hands over my face, knocking his away. "I don't know. It just started when you said you had to leave, and it won't stop. I did this last night when you went to your business dinner too. This isn't me. Sure, I cry, but not for no reason. Certainly not for no reason I can't do anything about."

He gently pries my hand away from my face and holds them. "I'm sorry I can't stay with you today. We have a lead we need to chase down before he moves somewhere else."

A slither of fear works its way through me, and I'm grateful he didn't say his name out loud. Not here in our bed, especially while we are both naked and he's touching me.

I nod once and shake my head, trying to give him a smile. "I'm sorry. It might just be hormones or something. I'm still tired and maybe just need some more sleep."

"Then rest today. I'll check on you later." He climbs off the bed, and I don't even hide the fact that I'm watching his beautiful round ass disappear into the closet.

He's beauty and brutality in perfect harmony. And I want both for as long as he'll keep me.

I roll over and snag my phone off the bedside table. It vibrated a few times while I cowered under the covers. I quickly click through to the read alerts and find a new text from the same number as last night.

Suddenly my stomach is in my throat, and I can barely draw in a breath. All thoughts of him nude and dripping wet flee my mind, leaving only naked fear. I open the text, but this time, it's a video.

Instead of waiting, I turn the volume to zero and glance at the closet. He's still dressing, so I have a minute. I hold my breath as I click the video and wait while it starts.

What pops on the screen isn't what I expected, yet it turns my stomach all the same. Bile rises in my throat, and I toss the phone into the covers and race to the bathroom. I barely make the toilet before I dry heave over the bowl a few times. The video images swimming in my head cause my body to try to expel them all over.

A cool hand on my neck, gathering my hair, breaks me from the vicious cycle, and I can sag back onto the tile. It's cold, and I let it cool me down, every part of me burning from fear, shame…I don't know.

"Are you sick? Do I need to call the doctor?" he asks gently.

I shake my head. "No. I'm fi—"

"If you say fine, I'm going to turn you over my knee and spank your ass until it's pink and you've spilled the truth. Don't fucking lie to me, Valentina."

It hurts to lie to him, and I don't want to, but I don't want him to see the video. If he sees me like that, he won't want me anymore. Who would?

I shake my head and lean back into his hand. It's wrapped completely around the base of my head as he cradles it.

"Angel," he prompts.

It turns my stomach all over again to think about him watching that disgusting video.

"My phone," I manage, unable to give him anything else.

He gently eases his hand away until he's sure I'm sitting up on my own, then heads back into the bedroom. A few seconds later, I hear glass shattering.

It takes me a moment to heave myself off the floor, with vertigo trying to pull me back down.

He's standing at the end of the bed, my phone clutched in his hands. There's a broken lamp on the floor, and I stare at it a few seconds too long. It's not that I fear he'll do that to me, just that I wish I could let go that way, break things, destroy them when something hurts me. It must feel good. Yet I can't. I wouldn't feel right, no matter how cathartic it might be.

"Put some clothes on, Angel. We'll have company in a moment."

I cross to the closet and throw on a T-shirt and a pair of black leggings. Quickly, I gather my hair up into a messy bun and gingerly step around the broken lamp. A few seconds later, a knock on the door reveals all of the five, followed closely by Kai.

They survey the scene, but he hands Vincent my cell phone. "Get what you can from this. Then gear up. We're going hunting."

"But, boss, we haven't finished our research."

He glares at all of them. "When you see what's on that thing, what that bastard sent her, and you don't want to go get him as bad as I do, then you can walk out the door now and don't bother coming back."

I step into his side and cling to his arm, trying to take his full attention off his men, and put some on me. He's always gentler with me when his temper rises, and I don't want to see any more of them hurt.

"Angel," he grits out between his teeth. "Get in bed and rest. Kai will be here with you while I'm gone."

He stares down his men. "Everyone else, get ready. We leave in fifteen minutes."

When he turns to face me, it's not the beauty winning today, it's the brutality, and Sal is going to feel the brunt of it.

I think about it for a moment and find I don't care one bit. This is what I bargained my life away for, and I'm finally going to get the revenge I'm owed.

The revenge Rose is owed.

## 33

## ADRIAN

*I* feel like a fucking idiot as I stare down the wooden dock toward the boats. Why didn't it occur to me to check if his family owned a boat? Of course he'd want to hide somewhere that offers a quick escape. Which is why my team and I sit here in the dark, car off, as the temperature inside the vehicle warms up without the A/C on.

If he saw us coming, I want him to settle back down, think everything is fine. That the black SUV we rolled up in is just another asshole with a too big boat out here in the middle of nowhere.

I owed Diavolo big for this tip or his coercion of my ex in telling me. Either way, I won't forget it if he ever needs something from me. With the object of this hunt so close, adrenaline is pumping through my system. I'm buzzing with it, and the anger is still festering from watching the fucking video he sent Val. I'm going to pluck out his eyeballs because he's seen her naked without her consent. I'm going to rip off his dick and throw it overboard before I drag my knife across his throat. A quick bullet is too good for him. I want him to suffer. I want him to hurt.

It won't make up for everything he's done to her, but at the very least if she asks me, I can tell her I made him scream before I put him out of his misery.

Andrea is my sniper today. Her small form is laid flat on top of a nearby boat. When she gives the signal, we all climb out of the car and head toward his yacht.

"If you find him, don't hurt him. That will be my pleasure. Hold him, incapacitate him, but nothing else." I meet the hard stares around the group. Everyone is ready for this. I'm fucking ready for this.

We ease up the dock, our boots silent and steady. We've done things like this a hundred times, a thousand times, and we move as one. It's why they are my five and no one else compares.

It only takes a few minutes to board the boat and find the hall leading up to the level he's lounging on. I motion at Vincent, who will grab him and drag him inside, so we don't have an audience. Alexie will find any staff on board and pay them well to take the day off. A part of me wonders if that's what Sal did the night he attacked Valentina. Paid everyone to look the other way.

The problem with sinning is…you must be ready to face the fallout. I'm more than ready to watch Sal's blood stain my clothing, my hands, all of it.

We ease into the bedroom with the balcony he's currently lounging on. I drag two chairs into the center of the room, pull my knife from my boot and hold it over my knee, then sit in one of the chairs and wait. A few seconds later, Vincent enters from the balcony, dragging a struggling Sal with him.

I wait until Vincent has him secured to the chair, the entire time staring down the scum who thinks beating on women will make him more of a man. Or maybe it was just her he liked to beat on because he couldn't fuck her like he imagined. Maybe when it came time to finish things, he couldn't get it up. That thought bolsters me as I lean forward, bracing my elbows on my knees.

"Hello Sal, I've been looking for you. You are surprisingly good at hiding. But what else can I expect from a fucking rat like you?"

Sal struggles against the ropes, but it's useless. He won't get free unless someone cuts him out of the bindings.

I wave my guys away. "Secure the perimeter and give us some privacy. We need to have a little chat."

They scatter as ordered, and Sal almost looks ready to piss himself and beg them to come back. If they only knew how much my men would enjoy helping me carve him up.

I lean forward, close enough now to touch him and trace the edge of my knife along the side of one cheek. My weapons are always honed, and he whimpers before the blood wells up and slides down his face, ruby red on his now bleached skin.

"Now that I have your attention, we're going to talk."

He swallows loud enough for me to hear it. "Ab-About what?"

"You may be a slimy asshole, but I don't think you're stupid. You know I'm here to talk about Valentina. My wife."

I watch his face shift as he takes in my words, and his fear turns to rage. "She was mine first. She belongs to me."

"I think Valentina would have something to say about that. She agreed to marry me in exchange for me killing you. And as you know, I never go back on my word."

His beady eyes narrow, and a lock of dirty hair falls across his forehead. "We can make a new deal. You keep her, don't kill me, and I'll find another wife. We can call it even. I lost something. You gained something…"

This fucker is actually trying to bargain with Valentina's life as if he has any say in it. The air around me sizzles, red-hot rage pumping deep in my veins. I shift in the chair, stand, and then slam my fist into his gut as hard as I can.

He wheezes out a breath and hunches over. I take my seat again, crossing my legs, and wait until he sits back up again. I let my rage fester, swallowing it down. I'm going to take my time and drag things out. It takes several minutes, but I have all day and night even to get this done.

"Tell me something, Sal. Once you had her tied down naked to her own bed, why didn't you finish it like you did with her cousin? Did you expect to be able to come back to the house and resume your engagement like nothing happened?"

He's shaking now, and a wet spot grows on his jeans. Good. He knows it's the end for him, and maybe he's finally accepting it. Still, for someone so brave to hurt Rose and Val the way he did, you would think he wouldn't piss his pants in front of danger. Then again, a man like myself standing in front of you is like placing a gun against your head and pulling the trigger.

"It wasn't...I didn't plan it. It was just...I had too much to drink, and I got jealous when I found her gone, and it happened. That's all. What does it matter? She survived."

Red coats my vision as I look at him. I want to shove his chair sideways and stomp on his skull until it gives a satisfying crack.

"She might have survived, but she'll never be the same. Because of you."

He breathes heavily now, barely able to keep his back up in the chair as I study him. Why on earth did her father think this man would make a suitable husband? Fucking anyone else would have been a better choice. *Anyone.* There are so many families in the society, some of them barely functional for lack of connections.

But it doesn't matter. None of it does because she belongs to me now, and there's nothing any of them can do to take her from me.

I shift forward once more, and he flinches away, knowing more pain is coming. The knife feels featherlight in my hand as I bring it across his face in a diagonal motion, cutting through the other side of his face so smoothly, like slicing silk. An ear-piercing scream fills the air, followed by a begging plea.

"Please, don't do this. We can work something out. I told you that you can have the bitch. I don't want her anyway. She's frigid and hated whenever I touched her."

I dig the blade in deep enough that it hits bone, leaving a hole in his cheek now. "You should watch what you say when I have this deep under your skin…I might get angry and slip."

He cries out as I sit back once more, my anger rolling in my gut, snapping the control I usually keep a tight hold on.

"You don't get a say about her life anymore. One more word indicating that, and I'll take a lot longer than I planned with you. I'll start with your toes and slice you up bit by bit until you change your fucking tune."

God, I fucking hate him so much. I'm shaking with it. I haven't felt this much unbalanced rage since I faced my father that night, the same knife in my hand.

"Let's get this straight, shall we? I'm going to kill you. It'll be painful because I want to please my wife. However, every word you say can determine how fast or slow this will go. As I said, I can slice you up bit by bit, or I can gut you in one quick stroke and leave you to bleed out."

His eyes go wide, and he starts shaking again. Fucking coward can't even face the death he's earned in the end. "What if I have information? Something you would want to know in exchange for my life?"

I shake my head. "Nothing you can tell me will compel me not to kill you tonight. Nothing at all."

When his eyes narrow and his spine straightens, I watch him closely. He thinks he knows something that can give him some leverage. I almost want to know what it is. But not enough to free him and not enough to let him live. Once his blood seeps into the floor, my debt to Val will be paid, and she'll be mine forever.

The thought bolsters me enough to send me scooting toward the bastard one more time. He flinches back and stammers out. "A little pussy isn't enough reason to start a war. You know, killing me outside of the season is an act of war, not only against my family but also against the council. Everyone will be on your ass."

I lean in and grab the back of his neck so I can whisper in his ear. "They'll have to find your body to prove it first."

Then I slide the knife into his fat stinking gut and enjoy the way he jerks in my grip.

I have blood seeping down my wrists and onto my shirt now, but I don't care. It'll prove it's done. She'll be able to see no one can take care of her like I can. No one can fucking give her what she needs like me.

He whimpers again, and I twist the knife, digging it in deeper. It won't take him long to die, and I'm okay with it. Right now, all I can think about is getting back to my angel.

"She's not worth it," he grits out.

I release his neck and jerk my knife roughly from his gut. "You want those to be your last words? I'd pick something more interesting, but it's up to you, I guess."

He groans and leans over in the chair. The dumbass doesn't even realize sitting that way will compress his wound and make him bleed out faster. "You have no idea what you're doing. She's a viper in your henhouse, and you don't even know?"

As if my angel could ever do anything to betray me. He obviously doesn't know a thing about her, and he never did.

It's a comforting thought as I watch the puddle of blood grow between our feet. I'm not leaving this spot until his heart stops beating. Otherwise, I won't be able to tell Val definitively he's gone for good.

I shoot a text to Alexei and tell him to find Sal's computer. If he has any more videos of Val on there, I want them all destroyed. Which reminds me.

I wipe my knife on his pants leg, cleaning it off, and then tuck it back into my boot.

Then I dig through his pants pocket to find his phone. This will need to be destroyed as well. No doubt he has some disgusting things on here.

"You are so fucked," he whispers, the light slowly leaving his eyes.

I sit back and straighten my jacket. "Aren't we all?"

He shakes his head, not even putting effort into it. Then with his last breath, he wheezes out, "She knows what happened to your mother."

## 34

## VALENTINA

*I* feel like an idiot, pacing back and forth in front of the elevators, my bare feet slapping on the time with every pass. Kai checked on me three times, and I waved him away. He's been worse with his hovering since that text came in from Sal. I've already forgotten it in my worry over Adrian.

What if Sal hurts him? What if he doesn't come back?

What if...

What if...

What if...

It's all I can think about as I pace and watch the number screen on top of the elevator for movement. No one has come up since the team left. I keep my phone tucked tight in my hands; the ringer turned up as high as I can make it. Once Kai took the information he needed from it, he returned it almost reluctantly.

Would it kill someone to call me and let me know Adrian is alive? Better yet, that Adrian is alive, and Sal is not.

I've never considered myself a vengeful person, but I decided to make an exception with Sal. He deserves nothing less than pain and suffering for all he's caused. And for all Adrian's sins, he's the perfect instrument to deliver the karma Sal earned all on his own.

A part of me wishes I were strong enough to be there for it, to watch. Even if the idea makes my fingers tingle with adrenaline, it also turns my stomach. Just being in the same room with him would make me puke.

I keep pacing, watching the number, waiting for it to move.

When the numbers begin moving, my pacing increases as I watch the screen. Each floor the screen eats up shoots a spike of fear through me. I'm not scared of Adrian. Even in the beginning, he's been nothing but honest with me. His moments of brutality have always been tempered with that honesty. I've learned he does nothing without a reason, and it's become a touchstone for me to understand what he might do next.

I keep pacing, watching, waiting until the elevator finally dings, and the doors slide open.

Inside, it's only him. But, at the same time, he's not the calm, collected man I've come to know. Something about the way he looks is unhinged. Hands braced behind him on the bars of the elevator, his white shirt is stained to the elbows in blood. It's also splattered all over his front. The jacket he'd left in is gone, and his usually perfectly styled hair is mussed and crusted with blood like he's been running his wet fingers through it.

God, I should be terrified of this dark god. He looks like something out of a horror film, yet I'm frozen, unable to look away.

He lifts his chin and locks eyes with me. When we first met, his eyes drew me in, a combination of soft and chilled. Right now, there's no softness in his gaze. No humanity, no give, nothing like the man I've come to understand over the months we've known each other.

I swallow hard, frozen in the center of the foyer.

He shoves away from the bar and steps into the penthouse. The doors whoosh closed behind him, trapping us together.

A part of me wants to run. A part of me is dying to know what happened. And a part of me wants to fall to my knees and give him anything he asks for.

When he reaches me, he stares down at me hard. The scent of blood wafts off him, sharp and metallic. "Have you been keeping secrets from me, Angel?"

My gulp is loud between us, and I can't take it back. I shake my head, unable to speak the words.

"Not good enough," he growls. "Try again. Have you been keeping secrets from me?"

"No," I squeak out. "I've told you everything. Not even things I shared with Rose."

He cocks his head, studying me. I hate him seeing my hesitation, seeing my fear. A long time ago, I accepted this is my life now. Facing this side of him is part of the job, and now that he's finally showing it to me, I can't flinch.

Or he'll never forgive me.

"I promise. I don't have any secrets from you," I say, my tone more confident despite my stomach tying itself in knots.

His fingers curve around my neck, not clutching, merely holding. "Should I believe you?"

"Why wouldn't you? Did Sal say something about me keeping a secret? How would he even know? I only spoke to him when I absolutely had to."

He walks me slowly toward the nearest wall, each step careful so I don't trip.

I don't understand his question or where this is going. Nor can I see past the almost feral look in his eyes as he stares me down.

"I promise," I repeat, hoping he'll believe me this time. "I promise. I don't want to keep secrets from you. I don't need to."

His fingers tighten a tiny bit, but I don't even flinch. There's no need. In my gut, I know he won't hurt me. And if this moment of...of...instability is what he needs, I can give him that.

I steel my spine and lift my chin. "Tell me what you want me to say. What you want to know. I'll tell you anything."

He hunches down to line our faces up. "He said you knew something about my mother's disappearance, about her death."

My voice trembles as I answer. "And you believe him?"

He snorts, his hand loosening now as he stands to his full height again. "He told me with his dying breath."

Fucking Sal. Of course he would use his last breath on Earth to continue to fuck up my life. He'd use it to turn the one person I care about against me.

His blood is slicked across my skin now, thanks to Adrian's hold and his proximity. I'm smeared with it, and right now, I don't fucking care. I want to revel in it. Rub it into my skin and laugh because he's gone, and I'm still standing, despite how hard he's worked to the contrary.

"I'm going to ask you once, and only once. Do you know anything about my mother or her death?"

I shake my head, but it's not much with his grip still on me. "No, of course not. The only thing I know about her is what you've shared with me. I don't know why Sal would say something like that except as his final 'fuck you' to me."

He slams me back into the wall, and my shoulders bounce against it. Not hard enough to hurt, just enough to rattle my bones. It's not even rough by my pain standards. "If I find out you're lying to me, that you know something, and you've lied to me this whole time…"

When he trails off, I arch my neck forward to catch his eyes again. "You'll what? Treat me the same way they did? Hit me? Hurt me?"

His jaw tightens, and he reaches out to rip the strap of my sundress. It sags down, baring my right breast to him. "Unlike Sal or your father, I follow through with my threats. There are worse things I can do to you than hurt you."

Despite his words and his grip. Despite the way he's holding me and handling me. Despite everything screaming at me to the contrary…I know he won't hurt me. Not the same way they did. Not even close.

"What do you want from me?" I whisper. "You asked a question, and I answered you."

His eyes are locked onto my bare skin, and he jerks the other strap of my other shoulder, leaving smears of blood from my shoulder to my bicep.

Then he drags the dress farther down so it slips off my hips and pools at my feet. I wait to see what he'll do next.

When he rips my panties off, one-handed, the fabric digs into my skin hard enough I know I'll have a bruise. But I don't make a sound.

I wait for the moment when my brain somehow leaves my body. An occurrence that happened regularly when Sal, or my father, put their hands on me, but it doesn't come. In fact, the opposite happens. It's as if every brush of his skin against mine only heightens my awareness of both him and my own body.

I reach out and unbutton his shirt, staring hard into his eyes, waiting for him to bat my fingers away. He doesn't, but he releases my neck so I can strip his bloodstained clothing off. Then for some reason, I go for his belt. My hands with a life of their own. My heart is pounding so loud in my ears I can't possibly hear anything else right now.

When I strip his belt, it's as if a switch is flipping in him. He steals it from my grasp and then yanks my hands behind me, wraps the belt tight, and cinches it to keep them immobile.

God, I should be terrified. But I'm so turned on I can feel the wetness on my thighs.

"You are not in charge," he whispers, leaning in. "Say it."

It takes me a couple of tries. "I'm not in charge."

He lines his body up with mine, dips down enough to probe my entrance with his cock, and then he's inside me. It's not gentle. I'm speared on him, my tiptoes barely on the ground before he lifts me by the hips and slams me hard into the wall.

He drops his forehead to my shoulder but then replaces it with his teeth. It's a sharp bite, not a gentle nip, and I moan in both pleasure and pain.

When he releases my shoulder, he chants, "You're mine," repeatedly.

I fight with the belt around my wrists, needing to touch him back, to hold on, give myself leverage. But there's no mercy in the way he pounds into me. He's slamming me into the wall, his hips working furiously, blood smeared all over both of us now. All I can do is close my eyes and lean my head back so it doesn't smack into his as he drags his teeth up to my neck to deliver another hard bite.

This one causes me to cry out. I can barely breathe with the intensity of it all. His fingers are so tight, his teeth digging into my flesh so hard I can't move, only breathe through it.

There's more pain than pleasure now, but I don't care. It's all for him. If he needs to take me this way, then I can handle it.

It hits me fast and hard. I was made to handle him at his worst. Honed for it by my years of abuse and trauma. I can take it like no one else could.

A surge of possessiveness rises in my chest, a lump squeezing everything tight. No one else will have him like this except me.

His movements start to get frantic, less smooth, more brutal with every stroke. I lean into the wall, waiting it out, even as pleasure starts to replace the pain. He switches the angle at the last second, his cock gliding against my clit now. I cry out, my eyes popping open.

He wraps one arm under my ass to lift me, and the other grips my neck. "Come now. Fucking come."

I shatter at his command. Everything inside me contracts tight around his cock. I come harder than I ever have, and he follows me a few seconds later, eyes still locked with mine, body still coiled tight against me.

When he slows, he still doesn't release me. "You belong to me," he says, his voice low, deep, thrumming things deep inside me hard enough to shoot another bolt of pleasure through me.

He eases me to the floor, pulling out of my body. "You belong to me, but if you ever betray me, I'll fucking kill you."

I nod my head, mainly because I'm afraid of the way my voice may sound and also because I'm past words. All I know is that I never want to be on the opposing side of Adrian.

## 35

## ADRIAN

*V*al doesn't respond but does acknowledge my words with a nod of her head. At some point, we make it to the shower, where I take my time washing both of us thoroughly. Sal's words refuse to leave my mind. I can't comprehend why he said what he did. A part of me wants to believe that it was his last chance at digging a knife into my chest, but then again, the criminal in me, the man hell-bent on avenging his mother's killer, tells me to believe him.

But doing that would put Val and me on opposite sides. It would make us enemies, worse than enemies, and I'm not certain I could fathom the outcome of such a thought. If she's lying... I clench my jaw and swallow the thought down.

Val is quiet, and once we're both dry, I lift her, carrying her in my arms until we reach the bed. When I place her gently against the sheets, her dark hair fans out in a halo above her head, and all I can do is stand there staring, drinking in her exquisite body.

I'm ravaged, starving for her, needing to touch her, taste her, possess her in every way possible. "I wish I had the patience to take my time with you, to caress you, and bring you to orgasm with my tongue and fingers before sinking deep inside you again, but if I'm being honest, I don't...I don't even have the power to be gentle with you. I won't ask for your forgiveness for what I've done and what I will do again. I need you, Valentina. You're mine, my wife, my fucking heartbeat."

Her pink tongue darts out over her bottom lip, and like a lion stalking its prey, I pounce. Nothing about the way I kiss her is gentle, my lips branding against hers while I connect our bodies with a feverish pace. The need to feel her warm heat around my cock was the only thing that matters in my mind. I take from her, holding her tight to my chest while spreading her thighs wider with my hips, sinking deeper inside her. She doesn't complain, even clawing my shoulders violently enough to leave marks.

She's heaven, and I'm hell, and when we collide, nothing will stand in our way.

"Fuck, tell me who you belong to," I growl, pressing my forehead against hers.

Val's eyes are hazy, and I can feel her pussy twitch, telling me she is close to her own release. "You. I'm yours… forever…" The words come out in a gasp as I pull all the way out, then slam back in. Val's mouth pops open, and her breath hitches, telling me I've hit the sensitive flesh at the top of her channel, and I know if I do that a couple more times, I'll spark an orgasm right out of her.

I move my hips in the same motion again and again until her pussy starts to convulse, the tightness alone making my eyes roll to the back of my head. I barely hold off coming, my balls aching and my cock screaming for release.

"Look at me, watch me…while I fuck you, while I mark you." I speak through my teeth and thread my fingers through her hair, tilting her head and forcing her attention on me. A low whimper escapes her lips, and I know she's sensitive from our previous fucking, but I can't seem to be bothered to care enough. She's the outlet to my rage, my punching bag, and I'm not finished with her yet.

"It's too much..." Her voice is hoarse, and I ignore the plea in it and slap the inside of her thigh, forcing her to hold herself open wider.

"I won't stop until you come again. I'll fuck you all night long until you're nothing more than a mess of tears, my cum, and flesh." Sweat beads on my brow and my muscles burn as I fuck her faster, harder, my touch firm enough to leave more bruises on her pale skin.

Like a bomb, Val comes again, her entire body shakes, and her tiny nails sink deep into my back, "Oh God, oh God..." She whimpers, and I let myself go then, letting every ounce of rage and pain out as I empty myself inside her.

My chest heaves as I try to catch my breath and roll off Val, pulling her into my chest, never letting our bodies disconnect. Neither of us says anything, but I can feel the weight of the silence around us. I want to tell her everything is going to be okay, but that would be a lie. Gently, I run my hands up and down her back until her breathing evens out, and I know she's fallen asleep.

I try to do the same, but sleep evades me. The thought of Val, someone I love having something to do with my mother's death, refuses to leave my mind. I'm not sure how much time passes but eventually, I drift off to sleep, my hold on Val unwavering.

It can't be but hours later when I'm woken by a light tap on the shoulder. I jerk awake and roll to stare at Kai. His face is pale, and he tips his head toward the door.

I ease my arms from around Valentina and carefully climb out of bed. Once I put on a robe, I head into the hall to find Kai leaning against the opposite wall. "What is it?"

"Vincent." His voice shakes, and I immediately know something is wrong. Nothing fazes Kai, not even my own threats to kill him.

I head toward the command room before he says anything else and find four of my five around the table. One is lying flat on top. I approach to find Andrea lying there, her clothing torn, her face beat up.

"Call the doctor," I order, reaching out to take her hand. But she jerks away as my hand gets close to hers.

"Don't touch me," she whispers.

I realize it's because she can't speak well, likely from the red rings around her neck. They look like rope burns.

I face the group now. "What the fuck happened?"

Kai takes the lead, as usual. "Vincent was attacked while cleaning up at the yacht. Sal's family found out what happened and launched an assault. They got to Andrea before Vincent's warning reached the rest of us."

I glance down at her again. "What the fuck did they do to her? And what about Vincent?"

"He's dead," Kai says, avoiding look at Andrea. "They delivered his head to the doorman a few minutes ago. I woke you as soon as I opened it. We've also gotten an invitation from the council."

I grimace and scan Andrea one more time, watching her breathe for my own peace of mind. Everyone in this room knows an invitation isn't voluntary.

"Get her to the hospital if she needs it. Whatever it takes. Do you know who exactly did these things?"

Kai shakes his head and scrubs his hands over his face. "It had to be Sal's uncles. They have a reputation for hating women and are known for their brutality."

A memory from last night flashes in my mind. The bruises I left on Valentina's skin in my anger and haste.

Shame eats at me, and I stalk away from the table to pour a glass of water and bring it back to Andrea.

She takes it, careful not to touch me, and sips it slowly. All I can do is stand there to give her comfort, and I hate it.

If I make a move to hit Sal's uncles now, it could make things worse with the council until I answer for Sal's death. I'm prepared to show them what Sal did to her, that his death was justified, but I won't be able to explain retaliation against his family too, no matter the provocation.

I turn and face Kai. "Get the doctor here, take her to her room, even if she fights all the fucking way there."

Over my shoulder, I order a pale Alexei, "Get dressed. We're going to see the council, then we hunt for the bastards who did this."

He nods, giving his sister one last look, and leaves the room. Kai is itching to go with me, I know it. But right now, I trust him to protect Valentina, and she must be protected at all costs.

I shove him into the door hard enough to slam it into the wall. "You watch over my angel. If anything happens to her while I'm gone, you'll be the next one to die."

## 36

## VALENTINA

This time, when he leaves to handle business, I don't watch the elevator. The past couple of days have made me see how much he needs me. That this isn't just a deal for him, and I'm not just the spoils of war. In time, maybe, I can become a real wife. The woman he needs leading at his side. It wasn't a role my mother ever got to fill for my father, but I have higher hopes for Adrian. When I speak, he listens to what I have to say, and that always melts my insides into a soupy puddle.

Dammit. I sit poking at my oatmeal, something bland for my recently rebelling stomach. I'm in love with him. It's the only explanation for how completely moony I feel about him right now.

I take another bite of my food and force myself to swallow. Adrian ordered me to eat and finish it all because my appetite has been off. I'm not feeling the food, but I want to see his face when I finish. It will please him, and I find I want that more than anything. Just to give him a reason to smile at me, to put his hands in my hair, lean my head back, and tell me I'm all his. So worth it if I don't throw everything up again.

I shove down one more small bite and wait, praying my belly settles. When it does, I force another. But my slow plan isn't working. Nausea rolls through me not in a wave but driving a damn steamroller.

I rush to the bathroom, knocking the chair over in the process. My knees sting from how hard I hit the floor to throw up everything I tried to keep down.

When the worst of it subsides, as do my dry heaves, I lay my head on the side of the toilet. I'll take a shower later. Right now, I just need to rest a second.

I've been feeling like crap for a week, a couple of weeks, I'm not sure. It used to just be after I ate, but now it seems to be constant. It makes me worry that Sal damaged something in me with his first assault. Something the doctor may have missed.

The second I mention it to Adrian, he'll call the doctor, and then there will be so many tests and more bed rest, and I'll go crazy with boredom as Adrian forces me to stay under the covers until well after I feel better. It seems easier to deal with it myself and wait things out. Maybe it's just a stomach bug or food poisoning? Does food poisoning last this long?

I mean, I can't be pregnant...right? It takes me a minute to remember the last time I had my period. It's been so long I can't even remember the exact date.

I shove off the toilet bowl and sit up straight, waiting for the room to stop spinning. When it doesn't, I stand, brush my teeth, wash my face, and stare at myself in the mirror. Outside of the nausea, I feel okay. Normal. My belly is still flattish, although I've put on a little weight from living with Adrian as he does force me to eat at least three meals a day.

Women know if they are pregnant? Right? They can feel it? I test my breasts, cupping them in my hands. They don't feel any more sensitive than usual. My body feels the same as always.

Shit. But I can't just assume it's all good and not check. However, the second I leave the penthouse, someone will be on my tail. Worse, Adrian will know exactly where I go and what I buy. I'm not ready to mention it to him until I know for sure. Not until I see the proof for myself.

There's only one option I have, and it's one I never wanted to take as it will get both of us in trouble if he spills later.

I grab my phone out of my pocket and request Kai meet me at my bedroom door.

He almost meets me there, questions in his eyes because I don't text him.

"Come in," I say, holding the door open wide.

"No, I'm good right here."

I sigh, grip the sleeve of his very expensive suit, and drag him into the room. "You don't want to be out in the open when I ask you this."

He waits, his face not too patient with me now. "What do you need?"

I cross to sit on the bed, my legs feeling wobbly now, my courage failing. No. I can't be scared of this, especially if I am pregnant.

I shift to face him. "I'm calling in your debt. You owe me your life, and I'm calling in the debt under the conditions no one knows what I'm about to ask you."

If I thought he looked wary before, it's nothing compared to his face now as he stares at me. "Really? This better be a doozy for you to pull that card."

I shrug and wait for his answer.

He glares a moment longer, then nods. "Fine. What is it?"

"You promise you won't say anything about this to Adrian?"

"I promise, for God's sake, Valentina, just tell me."

I relax a little bit. Kai might not be a saint, but I trust his word if he gives it. "I need you to go get me a pregnancy test. Maybe three just to be safe and completely sure."

I risk another glance at him. Now he doesn't look upset. He looks like I slapped him. "You." He stops and turns away, then spins back. "You think you're pregnant? Since when?"

I wave at the bathroom. "Now, just now. I haven't been feeling well, and then it hit me that I haven't had my period. But I don't want to say anything to Adrian until I know for sure one way or the other."

Kai's usually perfect skin is gray as he stares at me hard, like I'm about to spout another head or proclaim I'm pregnant with his boss's baby one more time. There's really nothing else to say so I wait for him to wrestle with this revelation.

Then he walks out without another word, leaving me staring at the empty doorway and semi-darkened hallway. Well, if he comes back with it, cool. If not, then I'll have to think of a plan B to get tested. Or tell Adrian and he'll help me do it. I just really don't want to give him more to worry about if it's just my imagination or my body still recovering from everything it's been through.

I lie back on the bed and focus on my breathing so I don't rush to the bathroom and puke again. To my surprise, less than ten minutes later, Kai walks in with a white shopping bag and tosses it onto the bed near my legs.

I carefully sit up in deference to my belly and then grab the bag and head into the bathroom. A part of me hopes he doesn't wait while I take these. Another part of me doesn't want to be alone when I find out the answer.

It doesn't matter...it's not like I'm going to drag Kai in here with me to witness things. I quickly strip the packaging from one of the tests and get it over with. Then I cap it, set it on the sink, and wait for the results.

My hands are shaking as I brace them on the counter next to the test. It just sits there, a little hourglass spinning on the tiny display screen while my insides are shredded with nerves and nausea.

When the screen blinks and changes, I gape down at the tiny black letters across it.

Pregnant.

I know I should take the other tests just to be a thousand percent sure, but I don't think I need to. It's the only logical explanation for how I've been feeling, and now that I see the results with my own eyes, it's almost as if I can feel it.

I press my hands over my lower belly. Of course, it's too early to physically feel a baby in there, but I still do it, waiting for nothing.

Quickly, I clean up the trash and hide the other tests behind some cleaner under the sink. Then I head back out to the bedroom even though I'm not ready to tell Kai the results yet. Besides, Adrian might get upset if Kai knows before he does.

Speaking of the father of my child...I smile at the thought and head down the hall. Maybe he's gotten back, and I can tell him now, get it over with so I don't have to keep it to myself any longer.

I head to the command room first, but it's empty. Not even the screen is on, so then I study the hall and remember he has an office a few doors down. There hasn't been a reason for me to go inside yet, but I still want to check and see if he's in there.

When I open the door, I catch a whiff of the spicy ginger scent I associate with him. It makes me want to stay there and breathe in his scent. I enter the room and flip on the light switch.

The office looks like him. It's minimalist and clean. Nothing out of place and nothing not necessary graces the space. There's a shelf with some pictures on it that draws my interest. Anxiety fills my veins, knowing I'm doing something I shouldn't. Despite it, I head over to scan them, needing to know more about him to feed this obsession I've developed.

I see one of him as a little boy. A picture of him and Kai as younger men. A smile tucks on my lips as I take in his handsome younger face. It's less weathered but also less shrewd, like he hadn't yet experienced many things in life.

I drag my gaze away to the last photo, and my heart stops mid beat. All the air whooshes from my lungs, leaving a cold emptiness behind. A million thoughts swirl around my head, forcing me to remember a night I'd rather forget. My hand shakes as I pick up the frame and study it closely, hoping, praying that I'm wrong. But there is no mistake. No matter how hard I look at the image.

"Hand me the gun, Valentina..."

I blink, the tears making my vision blurry, but I still know the woman in the image, next to a boy who is undoubtedly Adrian. She is the woman I saw when I was a little girl. The one lying in the bloody puddles reflecting the moonlight.

She has to be his mother. And I have no doubt he's been trying to figure out the mystery of her death since that day all those years ago.

Oh my God. Realization is setting in, and I'm shaking from head to toe, my heart pounding so hard in my chest it almost hurts.

The picture frame slips from my hands and hits the floor inches from my feet. The glass shatters into a million pieces, just like my life.

∼

Valentina and Adrian's story continues in
Promise to Keep

# ABOUT THE AUTHORS

**J.L. Beck** is a *USA Today* and international bestselling author who writes contemporary and dark romance. She is also one half of the author duo Beck & Hallman. Check out her Website to order Signed Paperbacks and special swag.

www.bleedingheartromance.com

∼

**Monica Corwin** is a New York Times and USA Today Bestselling author. She is an outspoken writer attempting to make romance accessible to everyone, no matter their preferences. As a Northern Ohioian, Monica enjoys snow drifts, three seasons of weather, and a dislike of Michigan football. Monica owns more books about King Arthur than should be strictly necessary. Also typewriters...lots and lots of typewriters.

You can find her on Facebook, Instagram and Twitter or check out her website.

www.monicacorwin.com

Made in the USA
Las Vegas, NV
03 January 2022